"I Don't Need You To Understand Me. Believe Me, You Don't Want To.

"But know this. I want you to keep your promise. I want to do right by this boy. I want to give him a home." Under the artificial light, his green eyes sparkled. "Come back with us to Leadeebrook."

A choking breath caught in her chest.

Infuriating. Insufferable. How dare he be charming and sincere now!

But although she'd like to deny it, the note of caring in his voice had touched her. Maybe there was an ounce of human in Jack Prescott, after all.

Sensing her slide, he moved to take over the carriage's handles. Still wary, she shook her head. "I'm not sure..."

But then he actually smiled—a damnable slow, bone-melting smile. "I think you are, Maddy." He began to walk, and when she relented and followed, he added, "I'll give you two weeks."

Dear Reader,

At a recent family wedding, I enjoyed the company of a wise lady who said, "If you're lucky enough to find the one person in this world who really 'gets who you are,' you should hang on tight and never let them go." Years earlier, this lady had met and married the man of *her* dreams. They were beyond suited and immeasurably happy, particularly when their beautiful dark-eyed daughter was born. Sadly, when that little girl was only four, her loving father was taken from them.

To look into this woman's eyes is to know she will love her husband forever. And logic says…if you've already gifted your heart to another, you haven't another to give. For some I believe this is true.

But not for all.

When his wife passed away, Jack Prescott—my hero in *Bargaining for Baby*—felt as if his life was over, too. Knowing that their unborn baby had died at the same time seemed to cement the headstone over those emotions. But when Jack's nephew needs a permanent guardian, the baby's temporary caregiver, Madison Tyler, finds an unsuspecting chink in this wealthy cowboy's cast-iron armor.

However, Jack is unwilling to gamble on love…as unwilling as Maddy is to live in Australia's harsh Outback. And yet an increasingly vulnerable part of this savvy city girl continues to wish that their mutual smoldering attraction will heat Jack's heart enough for him to realize that he still has love enough to give.

I hope you enjoy *Bargaining for Baby,* the latest story in Silhouette Desire's fabulous BILLIONAIRES AND BABIES series!

Best wishes,

Robyn

ROBYN GRADY

BARGAINING FOR BABY

Published by Silhouette Books
America's Publisher of Contemporary Romance

Recycling programs for this product may not exist in your area.

ISBN-13: 978-0-373-73028-5

BARGAINING FOR BABY

This edition published by arrangement with Harlequin Books S.A.

For questions and comments about the quality of this book please contact us at Customer_eCare@Harlequin.ca.

Visit Silhouette Books at www.eHarlequin.com

Printed in U.S.A.

Books by Robyn Grady

Silhouette Desire

The Magnate's Marriage Demand #1842
For Blackmail...or Pleasure #1860
Baby Bequest #1908
Bedded by Blackmail #1950
The Billionaire's Fake Engagement #1968
Bargaining for Baby #2015

ROBYN GRADY

left a fifteen-year career in television production knowing that the time was right to pursue her dream of writing romance. She adores cats, clever movies and spending time with her wonderful husband and their three precious daughters. Living on Australia's glorious Sunshine Coast, she says her perfect day includes a beach, a book and no laundry when she gets home.

Robyn loves to hear from readers. You can contact her at www.robyngrady.com.

This story is for Maxine, Katie and dear Aunt Jenn.
Three generations of smiles,
spunk and unfailing devotion.

With thanks to "Snow"
from Jondaryan Woolshed for your entertaining stories
and fascinating inside info, and also to my fabulous
Silhouette editor, Shana Smith.
Go us!

One

Jack Prescott wandered out from the public hospital room, his senses locked in a mind-numbing daze.

He'd received the call at ten that morning. He'd immediately jumped in his twin engine Piper Navajo and had flown to Sydney with his heart in his mouth the whole way. He and Dahlia hadn't spoken in three years. Now he'd missed the chance to say goodbye.

Or I'm sorry.

Through stinging eyes he took in the busy corridor. The air smelled of antiseptic and, beneath that, death. As of today, he was the last surviving Prescott and there wasn't a soul to blame but himself.

A passing doctor, deep in conversation, knocked Jack's shoulder. He swayed, braced his legs then spread out his remarkably steady hands to examine the calloused palms. How long before the nightmare truly hit? Before he fell to his knees and cursed this godless world? Where was the mercy? Dahlia had only been twenty-three.

A woman in the crowded waiting room caught his eye, her fair hair streaming over one side of a red summer dress. She held a bundle. A swaddled child.

Jack rubbed a gritty eye and refocused.

Beneath fluorescent lights, tears glistened on her lashes, and as she gazed back down the corridor at him, Jack wondered if they'd met before. When her mouth pressed into an I'm-so-sorry smile, his gut hollowed out.

One of Dahlia's friends.

But he wasn't sure he could put words together yet. Those token pleasantries like, "Oh, you knew my sister. Yes, she was very beautiful. Sorry, but I have to leave… make arrangements."

When the woman continued to wait, her pale hand supporting the baby's head, Jack couldn't avoid a meeting. He forced one leaden foot in front of the other and, an eternity later, stopped before her.

"You're Dahlia's brother, aren't you?" she asked. "You're Jack." Her flushed cheeks were tearstained, her nails bitten to the quick and her eyes…

Her eyes were periwinkle blue.

Jack sucked in a breath. When was the last time he'd noticed something like that? He wasn't sure he even knew the color of Tara's eyes. Perhaps he should take note when he got back. Not that theirs would be that kind of marriage. Not from his perspective, in any case.

After the death of his wife three years ago, Tara Anderson had spent increasing amounts of time at Leadeebrook, the Queensland sheep station where he lived. Jack had been slow to appreciate Tara's company; he wasn't much of one for talking these days. But as close as his deceased wife and this woman had once been, so he and Tara had become good friends, too.

Then, last week, Tara had offered more.

He'd been straight. He would never love another woman. His wedding band was threaded on a gold chain that never left his neck while his wife's ring lay at the foot of a photo he kept on his bedroom chest of drawers. Sue had not only been his wife, she'd been the other half of his soul. The better half.

Still Tara had put her argument forward. He needed someone steady in his life, she'd said. She needed someone to help manage her property. That had gotten Jack's attention. Twenty years ago, Jack's father buckled under hard times and had sold half his land to a neighbor, Tara's great-uncle. Later, he'd tried to buy the land back but Dwight Anderson wasn't interested.

After Sue's death, Jack's life had seemed pointless. He'd found no joy in occupations that had once caused the blood to charge hot and fast through his veins. Even throwing a saddle over Herc and giving his stallion free rein down a beloved Leadeebrook plain had seemed a chore. But the idea of fulfilling his father's dream of regaining those choice acres had offered Jack's darker days a glimmer of meaning.

Tara was a good woman and attractive by any man's standards. Perhaps they *could* help each other out. But before he married again, a matter needed sorting.

The human race relied on the power of maternal instinct—women wanted children and Tara would make an excellent mother. But he had no wish to become a father.

He'd made mistakes—one error unforgivable. He thought about it often and not only when he visited the tiny grave which lay beside his wife's in the Leadeebrook family plot. Having your heart ripped from your chest once was enough for any man. He wouldn't tempt fate by siring another child.

If Tara wanted a marriage of convenience, it would be without plans of a family. Although she had acquiesced with a nod when he'd told her as much, the mist in her eyes had said that she hoped he'd change his mind. Not tomorrow. Not ten years from now. On that point he was firm.

Jack's gaze had settled on the lightly-swaddled bundle when the woman in the red dress spoke again.

"Dahlia and I were friends," she murmured in a thready voice. "Good friends."

He inhaled, rushed a hand through hair that was overdue a cut and got his thoughts in order. "The doctor said it was a hit-and-run."

At a pedestrian crossing, of all places. Dahlia had died of internal injuries only minutes before he'd arrived. He'd touched her hand, still warm, and remembered how he'd taught her to ride Jasper, his first mount, and how he'd consoled her when her pet lamb had passed away. When she'd reached out and had begged him to understand...when his sister had needed him most...

"She regained consciousness briefly."

The woman's words took Jack off guard. The back of his knees caved and he sat, wishing he hadn't. Taking a seat implied he wanted to talk. What he wanted was to take off his boots, down a stiff Scotch and...

He looked up too quickly and the light faded in and out.

And *what?* Face forms, funeral directors, a choice of clothes for the coffin?

"She spoke to me before...before she slipped away." The woman's lips were full and pink now, the bottom trembling the barest amount. "I'm Madison Tyler." She repositioned the baby and lowered to sit beside him. "Friends call me Maddy."

He swallowed hard against a closed, dry throat. "You said she regained consciousness…spoke to you."

Surely not about him. Dahlia had been a wreck after their parents' deaths. Not even his wife's patience and support had gotten through to her. That final night, Dahlia had shouted she didn't want another thing to do with her brother, his stupid rules or Leadeebrook. She'd come to Sue's funeral but he'd been too dazed to speak. Over the years, he'd received Christmas cards, but no forwarding address.

His hands clenched on his thighs.

Lord and Holy Father, he should have set pride aside and *found* her. Protected her. Brought her back home.

The baby stirred and Jack took in the sleeping face, the shadow of tiny lashes on plump healthy cheeks. So new and full of promise.

Full of life.

Clearing his mind and the thickness from his throat, he found his feet and the bulk of his control.

"We can talk at the wake, Miss…"

"Maddy."

He drew his wallet from his back pocket and dug out a card. "I'll see that the notices are posted. You can get me on this number if there's anything."

Finding her feet, too, she searched his eyes.

"I need to speak with you, Jack. I need to speak with you now." She stole a glance at her baby. "I didn't know… Well, Dahlia hadn't spoken about you before."

When her gaze meshed with his again, her eyes were round and pleading, as if she wanted an explanation. She seemed sweet enough, and understandably shaken, but whatever Dahlia had said, he wasn't about to justify himself to a stranger. To anyone, for that matter.

His gaze broke away as he waved the card. "I really ought to go."

"She told me that she loved you," she blurted out, jerking half a step closer. "That she forgave you."

Bent over, placing his card on the chair, he stopped, clamped his eyes shut and willed away the thumping heartbeat in his ears. He wanted this week to be over. Wanted to get back home. Back to his land. What he knew. What he could keep.

He straightened slowly and kicked up a firm chin. The baby was stirring, beginning to squeak and complain. A part of Jack was drawn to the sound while another only wanted to plug his ears and stalk away. The last straw would be to hear an infant cry.

Exhaling, he shoved the wallet in his back pocket. "There's nothing you can do here. You should get that baby home."

"I'm trying."

When she purposely held his gaze, he shook his head then shrugged. "Sorry. You've lost me."

But she only rolled her teeth over her bottom lip, her eyes huge and…

Frightened?

He assessed her classic bone structure—flawless porcelain complexion, the delicate curve of her jaw—and, despite the day, an instinctive flicker of arousal licked over his skin.

Was she implying that the child was his?

Some time after his wife's death, concerned friends had tried to lure him out from behind the walls he'd built around himself. They'd invite him to Sydney, to introduce him to suitable ladies within their circles. Although his heart had remained closed, there'd been a time or two he'd invited a date back to his inner city penthouse.

Was that why this woman seemed familiar? Had he slept with her sometime in the past?

He shucked back tense shoulders.

No. He'd have remembered those lips.

"Look, Miss—"

"Maddy."

He spared a tight smile. "Maddy. Neither of us is in any mood for games. Whatever you have to say, I'd appreciate it if you would spit it out."

She didn't flinch or coil away from his candor. Rather her expression took on a steely air.

"Dahlia left the baby with me today," she said. "He's not my son. This baby is your nephew."

Two beats of roaring silence passed before her words hit his chest, winding him as surely as if he'd been rammed by a twenty-foot log. He blinked rapidly, tried to find his breath. He must've heard wrong.

"That's…not possible."

A tear rolled down her cheek, catching and beading on the bunny blanket's blue hood while her periwinkle eyes gleamed with quiet strength.

"Your sister's last wish was for me to introduce you to one another. She wanted you to take him, Jack. Take him home with you to Leadeebrook."

Two

Fifteen minutes later, sitting across the table from Jack Prescott, Maddy brought the china cup to her lips, certain that she'd never seen anyone look more drawn.

Or more handsome.

With the shadow on his strong square jaw—as well as his demeanor—growing darker by the minute, his teaspoon click-clacked as he stirred sugar into his cup.

Over the intercom, someone called for Dr. Grant to go to ward 10. An elderly woman at a nearby table smiled at the baby before tasting her scone. By the cashier, a nurse dropped a full plate. The clattering echo bounced off the walls yet Jack Prescott seemed oblivious to it all. His hooded yet intense gaze was focused only inward.

From beneath her lashes, Maddy analyzed the planes of his rugged, Hollywood face—the cleft chin, the straight proud nose. How he managed to look both passionate and detached at the same time she couldn't guess. She sensed a fierce, almost frightening energy broiling beneath the mask. He was the kind of man who could single-handedly beat a bushfire in forty knot gusts and refuse to let anything he cared for suffer or die.

The million dollar question was: What *did* Jack Prescott care about? He'd barely looked at the baby, the orphaned darling he'd only just met. The man sitting at this table seemed to be made of stone, a perfect enigma. She might never know why Dahlia had excluded her brother from her life. If it weren't for little Beau, Maddy wouldn't *want* to know.

Jack settled his cup in its saucer, and then slid a bland expression toward the baby, who was settled again, asleep on his side in the carriage with a tiny fist bunched up near his button nose. Jack had been the one to suggest coffee, but after so long of a silence, Maddy couldn't stand his chilly calm a moment more. She had a task to complete—a promise to keep—and a finite amount of time in which to do it.

"Dahlia was a great mother," she told him. "She'd finished her degree in business marketing before the baby was born. She was taking a year off before finding and settling down to a good job." Maddy's gaze dropped to her cup as a withering feeling fell through her center. Now was the time to say it. Now was the time to confess.

"Dahlia had barely been out of the apartment since bringing him home," she went on. "I'd talked her into going to the hairdressers, having her nails done—"

Maddy's stomach muscles gripped and she grimaced under the weight of her guilt.

If she hadn't suggested it, hadn't made the appointment and practically pushed her friend out the door, Dahlia would still be alive. This baby would still have his mother and have no need to rely on this brusque man who seemed set on ignoring him.

"He's three months old today," she added, in case he was interested, but Jack only concentrated on stirring more sugar into his drink.

Maddy blinked several times then pushed her cup away and glanced, sick at heart, around the noisy room. This exchange was never going to be easy, but could it have gone any worse? What was she supposed to do now? The man was as sensitive as a slab of cold steel.

"Where's the father?"

Maddy jumped at his graveled question. But the query was an obvious one, even if he wouldn't like the answer.

She lowered her voice. "Dahlia was the victim of a rape." His face darkened before he swore and shoveled a hand though hair black as ink. "And before you ask," she continued, "she didn't report it."

Flecks of gold ignited in the depths of his hostile green eyes. "Why the hell not?"

"Does it matter now?"

Like so many in her situation, Dahlia hadn't wanted the misery of a trial. She hadn't known her assailant and preferred to keep it that way. She'd needed to heal as best she could and bury the horror as well as the hurt. Then Dahlia had discovered she was pregnant.

Choking on raw emotion, Maddy focused and straightened her spine. "What matters is she had a beautiful baby." This bright little boy she'd loved very much.

Jack studied the baby, the single line between his dark brows deepening as a pulse ticked at one side of thick, tanned neck. His next question was a grudging growl.

"What's his name?"

"Beauford James."

Jack Prescott's nostrils flared and his gaze slid away.

Maddy smothered a humorless laugh. Was this man a *machine?* Certainly these were special circumstances—he'd lost his only sibling today. But did he *ever* deign to show the world any emotion other than irritation?

Hot tears pricked behind Maddy's eyes as her hand tightened around her cup and rising emotion blocked off her air. She couldn't hold her tongue. No decent person would. Nothing had mattered more in her life than the outcome of this meeting—fulfilling the promise that she'd made—and if she had to brush an over-indulged ego the wrong way to get results, then by God, that's precisely what she'd do.

"He's your flesh and blood," she challenged. "Don't you want to pick him up and hold him?"

Promise him everything will be all right? That he'll be safe?

A dreadful thought struck and the fine hairs on her arms stood up at the same time as she slumped back. "Or would you rather he go straight to foster care?"

Not that she would let that happen. She'd take Beau herself first. Her own mother had died when Maddy was five. Growing up she'd longed for someone to braid her hair in the morning, burrow down beneath the covers with and read to her at night.

Maddy's father was a good man but obsessed with his business—sometimes it seemed as if Tyler Advertising was more Drew Tyler's child than his only daughter. He ran his corporate castle with an iron fist and didn't see a place on its staff for a "delicate girl" like Maddy. She disagreed. After serious and extended debate, she'd won and had gone to work at the firm.

These past weeks her father had become understandably edgy over his daughter closing her first big solo deal. Beneath the brave face, Maddy was nervous, too. But, come hell or high water, she'd have the signatures she needed and by the date promised. One month from today.

No one would guess how painfully shy she'd been as a girl, how hard she'd worked on her flaws in order to reflect her father's celebrated style of business savvy and determination. Now, not a day went by that Drew didn't in some way acknowledge his daughter's efforts. Still, there were times she wished she'd known a mother's love.

Her gaze fell to the baby.

How would this little one fare?

Jack's long, tanned fingers reached for the sugar bowl. "I don't recall saying I wouldn't take him," he drawled.

"You hardly seem gripped by the idea." Maddy slid back and one inky black brow arched.

"You'd do better not to be so hostile," he said.

"You'd do better not to be such a cold fish."

While her heart pumped madly, his expression didn't change. Those lidded sexy-as-sin eyes merely peered into hers until a not unpleasant shiver rippled over her skin, heating her from crown to curling-toe.

Blinking rapidly, she shifted back into the hard plastic seat.

Not only was this man dripping with bad-boy sex appeal, in that last point he'd been right. He might be as demonstrative as a stunned salmon, but now was the time for calm, not commotion. No matter how difficult, for the baby's sake, she must keep her emotions in check.

All of them.

Maddy loosened the grip on her cup and found the calm place inside that served her well in trying situations.

"This day has been a shock for us both," she admitted, "but, believe me, I only have one objective in mind, and that's to make certain Beau is cared for the way Dahlia would've wanted." She leaned in again, praying her heart would be there for him to see in her eyes. "Jack...he needs you."

A muscle in his cheek flexed twice. "So it would seem."

When he downed the rest of his coffee that must be three parts sugar and stone cold by now, Maddy's hackles went up.

All her life she'd mingled with powerful men, business associates from her father's advertising firm, influential patriarchs of the boys she'd dated in university. She'd seen an investment banker multimillionaire for a while. But never had she met anyone who stirred such strong emotions within her.

Both negative and shamelessly positive.

The hot pulse that kicked off low and deep inside whenever she looked at Jack Prescott was real. His presence was so commanding, despite the day, she couldn't help but be intrigued. The breadth of his shoulders, the strength in his neck...his man-of-the-land build was magnificent. His gestures, his speech, everything about him whispered confidence. Intelligence. Superiority.

Detachment.

The angel asleep in that carriage hadn't another living relative left in the world. Yet this specimen of masculine perfection, this emotional *ice man,* couldn't bring himself to even ask to hold him. She wouldn't have been able to leave Beau with his uncle and simply walk away, even if she had a choice.

Her stomach churning, Maddy nudged the blanket higher on the baby's shoulder and kept her eyes on the soft rise and fall of his little chest. There was never going to be a right time. Might as well bite the bullet and get the final bombshell out in the open.

"There's something else I need to say," she murmured. "About a promise I made."

Jack consulted his Omega platinum wristwatch. "I'm listening."

"I promised that I wouldn't hand Beau over until you were ready."

While her heart jack hammered against her ribs, the man across from her slowly frowned and folded his arms. Eventually he tugged his ear.

"I admit it'll take time to adjust to the idea of having..." His words ran dry, but then he cleared his throat and put more grunt into his voice. "You only need to know that I don't renege on my responsibilities. My nephew won't want for a thing."

It wasn't enough. If he'd greeted the baby with open arms, she'd still need to keep her word. She'd promised on her mother's grave to make certain Beau was settled.

Turning from the baby, Maddy clasped her hands in her lap and met Jack's superior gaze square on.

"I promised Dahlia that I'd stay with Beau until you were comfortable with each other. I imagine you have plenty of room," she hastened to add, "and I'm happy to pay for any expenses incurred."

The haunting cool in his eyes turned to flickering questions. He cocked his head and a lock of black hair fell over his suntanned brow while the corners of his mouth lifted in a parody of a smile.

"I need to have my ears checked. Am I getting this straight? You're inviting yourself to stay with me?"

"I'm not inviting myself anywhere. I'm passing on your sister's wishes. I'm telling you I made a promise."

"Well, it won't work." He shook his head, almost amused. "Not in a million years."

Maddy drew back her shoulders. He might be big. He

might be intimidating. But if he thought *he* was inflexible, these days stubborn was her middle name.

She'd try a different tack.

"This baby knows me. I know him. His routine, his cries." *Hopefully what to do when he wakes up, wanting his mummy.* "It's in your best interest to let me help you both adjust."

"I'll have help."

He'd said it without blinking and her heart missed several beats.

Dahlia said this morning that she'd followed what she could of her brother's life, really only that he still lived at Leadeebrook and hadn't remarried since the death of his wife. Of course he would need to hire a nanny. But what kind of person would be looking after Beau? Would she be severe and by-the-book or would she use her heart as well as her skills? Would she encourage him with gentle words of praise, or rap his knuckles if he forgot to say please?

"Miss Tyler…" A glimmer of warmth shone in his eyes when he amended, "Maddy. Are you sure this isn't more about your inability to let go?"

A dark emotion she couldn't name spiked and she kicked her chin up. "Rest assured, if I could be certain he'd be happy, if I could walk away with a clear conscience, nothing would please me more than to give you both my blessing."

That glimmer froze over. "Only I don't need your blessing, do I?"

Given that he was this baby's sole surviving relative, she conceded, "I suppose you don't. But then you don't appear to need anything—" she dammed her words then let them spill out anyway "—particularly this hassle." Lashing her arms over her chest, she challenged his hard gaze. "Am I right?"

When he didn't answer—merely assessed her with those striking gold-flecked eyes—her core contracted around a hot glowing knot. Before the heat flared any higher, she doused the flame and pushed to her feet.

Walking out wouldn't help matters, but she'd had all she could take for one day. The term *animal magnetism* was invented for this man: Jack Prescott was uniquely, powerfully attractive, but no way was he human. And before she left, damned if she wouldn't tell him just that.

"I respected Dahlia," she got out over the painful lump in her throat. "I loved her like a sister, but I can't imagine what she was thinking choosing you to care for this precious child."

With unshed tears burning her eyes, Maddy readied the carriage and headed for the exit. Jack called her name, but he could go to hell. He was no more interested in this baby's welfare than she cared what team won the national dart competition. If he was so uninspired, he could fly back to the scorched red plains of the Australian outback and leave Beau here in civilization with her. No child should need to grow up in a wasteland anyway.

One moment the cafeteria doorway was an arm's length away, the next Jack's impressive frame was blocking her escape. His legs braced shoulder-width apart, he deliberately set his fists low on his hips.

Maddy huffed over a smirk.

Well, whaddaya know. I got a reaction.

His head slanted. "Where are you going?"

"What do you care?"

She angled the carriage to swerve around him, but he

shifted to block her path again. "I care more than you'll ever know."

But she was done with words. She moved again. He moved, too. Narrowing her eyes, she let out a jaded sigh. "I've tried being reasonable. I tried understanding. I've even tried appealing to your better nature. Now I give in. You beat me, Jack Prescott." She raised her hands. "You win."

"I didn't realize we were in competition."

Oh, please. "Only from the moment you laid eyes on me." He'd wanted her gone? He could clap himself on the back. *Mission accomplished.* If Dahlia had heard this exchange, she wouldn't blame her friend for walking out.

"So, you've made up your mind?" he asked and she smiled sweetly.

"If you'd kindly step aside."

"And the baby?"

"We both know how you feel about raising Beau." It was in every curl of his lip.

A sardonic grin tugged one corner of his mouth. "You think you have me figured out, don't you?"

"I wish I could say I had the slightest interest, but I'm afraid I have as much curiosity about your workings as you've shown toward your nephew today."

While she simmered inside, his gaze drilled hers for a protracted, tense moment before his regal bearing loosened slightly. "What are you proposing?"

"What you're dying to have me propose. I'll relieve you of any obligation and take Beau off your hands." She would raise him, and show him love and loyalty and a million other values of which this man was clearly devoid. She'd work it out somehow with her job, with her father. "And if you're worried that I'll ask for financial support, don't be. I'd rather wash dishes fifteen hours a day than take one penny from you."

The air heated more, crackling and sparking between them before those big bronzed hands lowered from his belt.

"How are you in small aircraft?"

Her mouth fell open then snapped shut again. What was he talking about? Hadn't he heard a word she'd said?

"I flew down in a twin engine," he went on. "There's room for passengers but some people get queasy about small planes." His mouth twitched. "Though I have a feeling you're not the queasy type."

"I meant what I said—"

"You meant what you said to Dahlia," he cut in, but then dropped his voice as a curious older couple wove around them. "I don't need you to understand me. Believe me, you don't want to. But know this. I want you to keep your promise. I want to do right by this boy. I want to give him a home." Under the artificial light, his green eyes sparkled. "Come back with us to Leadeebrook."

A choking breath caught in her chest.

Infuriating. Insufferable. How dare he be charming and sincere now!

But, although she'd like to deny it, the note of caring in his voice had touched her. Maybe there was an ounce of human in Jack Prescott, after all.

Sensing her slide, he moved to take over the carriage's handles. Still wary, she shook her head. "I'm not sure…"

But then he actually smiled—a damnable slow, bone-melting smile. "I think you are, Maddy." He began to walk and when she relented and followed, he added, "You've got two weeks."

Three

Four days later, Maddy clutched her passenger seat armrest as Jack Prescott's private aircraft touched down on Leadeebrook Station's unsealed airstrip.

Jack had given her two weeks to fulfil her promise to Dahlia. Two weeks, no more, to have Beau settled in his new home with his new guardian. She would've liked more time, or at least the option to discuss the possibility of an extension should she deem one necessary. But, in the short period she'd known Jack, of one thing she was certain—he didn't speak for the sake of hearing his own voice. He was prepared to tolerate her company for precisely fourteen days. She supposed she ought to be grateful he'd seen the light and had relented at all.

When she stepped out from the plane onto the floor of the open ended hanger, the heat hit her like the long breath off a fire. The urge to spin around and crawl back inside the cool of the sumptuous cabin was overwhelming.

Instead she gritted her teeth and edged out into the blinding white sunshine.

Shading her brow, she cast a curious glance around the endless isolated plains—miles of bleached dry grass, parched scattered gum trees, lazy rolling hills shimmering a hazy purple in the distance.

She worked her dry throat enough to swallow.

Practically any part of Australia could get hot enough to fry eggs on the pavement. A serious summer's day in Sydney could rival a stint in a sauna. But out here the heat was different—bone dry—as if any sign of moisture would evaporate off a person's skin as soon as it surfaced. Within a week she'd be as dehydrated as the lifeless leaves hanging from those tired eucalypts.

Something bit her calf. She slapped at a beast of a fly then cringed at the red dust clinging to her new Keds. Who would choose to live in this godforsaken wilderness? No wonder Dahlia had escaped.

"Welcome to Leadeebrook."

At the husky voice at her back, Maddy angled around. Jack had followed her off the plane, aviator sunglasses perched upon his proud nose, carrying the diaper bag with one arm and Beau in the other.

Grinning, Maddy set her hands on her hips.

Heck, her iron cowboy looked almost relaxed. Nestled against that hard chest, Beau certainly did, which was a good sign. She'd been so worried.

Since the accident, she'd taken time off work to be with the baby 24/7. While her father sympathized with the situation, he wasn't pleased that his star junior account executive had asked for a leave of absence. He was less pleased when she'd told him she needed an additional two weeks out of the office. He needed the national deal she was working on bagged, no excuses.

She'd worked to reassure him. The Pompadour Shoe and Accessory campaign and media schedule were a wink away from being polished to a "simply-sign-here" shine. She'd be back in plenty of time to tidy loose ends. But these two weeks belonged to Beau, and today, in this unfamiliar environment, she felt more responsible for that baby than she could ever have dreamed possible.

When Jack had insisted she leave the plane cabin first—that he would bring the sleeping baby out directly—she'd automatically gone to object. She'd grown so used to the weight of him, his powdery scent, his smile; she ought to be the one to carry the baby out to greet his new home. But her friend's final request had echoed again in Maddy's mind.

Her job here was to do everything in her power to nurture an environment in which these two could connect and she could walk away knowing that Beau would be happy and cared for…that, God willing, he'd be loved and appreciated for the special little person he was.

That meant stepping back.

Watching the baby blink open his sleepy blue eyes and frown questioningly up into Jack's suntanned face—seeing Jack shift the nappy bag higher on his arm in order to push the sunglasses back into his thick hair and return the curious look—a cord in Maddy's chest pulled tight.

There'd been a slight shift in Jack's attitude toward his nephew. It seemed that now the funeral was behind them, he'd begun to show a tentative interest in his ward. Tender looks. Once the barest hint of a smile. But this was the first time he'd carried the baby, and while his wall was still steadfastly up, hopefully these small steps were seeds that would grow into a lasting, mutually loving relationship. Maybe, despite her misgivings and the sinking feeling that had minced around in Maddy's belly the whole uncommunicative flight here, Dahlia's wish would come true. That by the time she returned to Sydney, this aloof lone cowboy would have opened up, not only his home but also his heart to the person who needed him most.

Maddy stepped forward. But rather than take the baby, she cupped Beau's soft warm crown and smiled.

"He's awake. I can't believe he slept the whole flight."

"Isn't that what babies do? Sleep?"

When Jack's dubious gaze met hers, a frisson of awareness shot like the crack of a pistol through her blood. His sex appeal went beyond powerful; it was mesmerizing. The urge to tip close and savor that hypnotic lure was near irresistible.

Clearly Jack didn't mean for her to melt whenever they came within arm's distance. He had not the slightest interest in her *that* way. But she could do without him looking at her like that—as if she puzzled or intrigued him. As if he needed to know how her mouth might fit beneath his.

Her insides twinged and, guilty, she averted her gaze.

Those kinds of feelings were not only misplaced, they were dangerous. Next thing, she'd be looking at him cross-eyed. If she wanted to survive the following days—and nights—alone out here in Nowheresville with this maddeningly tempting man, she'd best make a pact with herself right now.

No matter how strong the tug—no matter what words Jack said, or smiles Jack gave—she'd allow nothing other than these searing outback temperatures to tamper with her body heat.

Composure restored, she straightened and replied, "Babies do a little more than sleep."

"Sure. They eat."

When he cocked a brow and managed to look both naive and sexier still, she couldn't contain a grin. "You know nothing about babies, do you?"

He dropped the glasses back onto his nose. "Not if lambs don't count."

He headed off, his focus hooked on the two-story homestead a walk away. Maddy's step slowed as she took a moment to drink in the place that Jack called home. Or, perhaps, a better word might be *palace*.

Leadeebrook Homestead was an impressive structure that radiated both elegance and a proud sense of endurance. Skirts of yesteryear lace ironwork surrounded both levels of veranda. Bordered by decorative masonry arches, large stately windows peered down at her. The lower floor sprawled out on either side in grand style. Maddy envisaged lavish drawing rooms, perhaps a ballroom, definitely a contemporary office, equipped with every convenience and littered with sheep stud memorabilia. The overall picture substantiated what she'd heard about the days when the country's wealth and glory had ridden on a sheep's back. Maddy could imagine the menagerie of characters who'd frequented its floors and the thrilling early settler stories they could tell.

A flock of pink galahs squawked overhead. She cast another resigned glance around the sun-scorched scene and hurried to catch up.

When a churning tunnel of disturbed dirt appeared in the near distance, Maddy wasn't certain what it meant. She shaded her eyes and narrowed her focus. A rangy dog was tearing up the track toward them leaving a swirling plume of dust in its wake.

A dart of panic hit her in the ribs.

Dogs were unpredictable. They could be savage. She didn't like being around them and she liked Beau being around them less. But this was a sheep station. Why hadn't she thought ahead? Of course there'd be a sheep dog. Maybe two or three.

As the dog sped closer, a hot-cold chill rippled up her spine. Maddy's fingers began to tingle and her breathing shallowed out. She hadn't had a full-blown panic attack in years. Now she recognized the signs and took measures to control them.

Regulate your breathing. Think calm thoughts.

But that comet of a dog kept coming. When the space between them shortened to within feet, she clenched her muscles, ready to dive and shield the baby. If someone was going to be slammed, it wouldn't be Beau.

At the last moment, the dog peeled away. Maddy's soaring adrenaline levels dipped and she slumped with relief—until a shiver fluttered up her limbs and her senses heightened again.

She carefully turned.

Head low, the dog was crouching up behind them. They were being stalked, like deer by a practiced wolf.

Jack growled out a playful "Git here, you," and, ears alert, the dog shot up to her master's side, her dark eyes blind with adoration and anticipation as she waited for the next order.

Shuddering out a shaky breath, Maddy worked to gather herself and force her leaden feet forward while Jack hoisted the baby higher against his chest.

"Meet Nell," he said.

Maddy preferred not to. Nevertheless she nodded curtly at the dog with the lolling pink tongue and penetrating brown eyes while keeping her distance. "Hello, Nell."

Jack paused to give her a dirty look. "You don't like dogs?"

"Let's say dogs don't like me." She had no intention

of explaining further. "She seems to hang off your every word."

"Nell's a working dog." A muscle ticked in his square, shadowed jaw. "Or she was."

Maddy tilted her head. *Was* a working dog. Had Nell had an accident? God knows she seemed agile enough. But Maddy had a more important question to ask.

"Is Nell good with children?"

Jack picked up his pace. "How should I know?"

As they moved toward the house, Nell trotted wide circles to manage her human flock, every so often darting up behind to nose their heels. Although Maddy remained outwardly calm, suffocating tendrils twined around her throat. But clearly this Border collie was well-trained. There was nothing to fear, for herself or the baby. Her falling blood pressure—her tingling brain—was an automatic physiological response to past stimuli. Just because she'd been mauled by a dog many years ago didn't mean it would happen again.

Breathe deeply. Calm thoughts.

As Nell flew past, the dog's tail brushed her wrist. Maddy's anxiety meter lurched again and she coughed out a nervous laugh.

"I have to say, I'm feeling a little like a lamb chop."

Jack flattened his lips and a sharp whistle echoed out over the plains. When he nodded ahead, Nell tore off. Maddy spluttered as more dust clouded her vision and filled her lungs. Fine grains of dirt crunched between her teeth. She needed a bath *and* a drink—a big fat Cosmopolitan with an extra shot of everything.

His broad shoulders rolling, Jack glanced across and measured her up. "There's reception for your cell phone if you need it."

"That's nice to know. Thanks."

"You bring any jeans?"

"Of course." The new season's latest cut.

"Good."

Goosebumps erupted down her arms. Something in his assured tone worried her. "Why good?"

"You can't ride in a dress."

She blinked. *Ride?*

Then she laughed. "Oh, I don't ride." Certainly not horses. She hadn't even swung a leg over a bicycle since that day when she was twelve.

Jack's brows fell together. "You don't like horses either?"

Her brows fell, too. "I didn't realize it was a federal offense."

Then again she was "out west." He probably slept with his saddle tucked under one arm and his Akubra glued to his head.

While she smacked another fly, Jack sucked air in between his teeth. "So you're not a fan of animals."

"Not up close."

He grunted. "What *do* you like?"

"I like the theater. I like chocolate custard. I like rainy days when I know I don't have to get up."

"Are there many days you don't get out of bed?"

She gave him a narrow-eyed look. Was he serious? His tone and expression were so dry, she couldn't tell.

"What I mean," she explained in an overly patient tone, "is that I love to prop myself up against a bank of pillows, snuggle down and read when rain's falling on the roof."

He grunted again—or was that growled—and kept his strides long while she wiped her damp brow and cringed as sweat trickled down the dent in her back. Up ahead, the homestead shimmered like an extravagant desert mirage.

A few minutes yet before they reached shade. But the sun was behind them, the baby seemed settled and the dog had disappeared. On his own turf, Jack seemed to be opening up, a little. Time to get to know more about Beau's legal guardian.

"What about you?"

"What about me?"

She rolled her eyes. She would *never* be able to talk to this man.

"Do you read, Jack?"

"No," he stated in a deep and definite voice. "I don't read."

Maddy blinked. She might have asked him if he wore pink stockings on a Saturday night. "But you do ride." He kept striding and she gave a skip to keep up. Okay. Obvious answer. No need to reply.

"I imagine you'll teach Beau to ride, too, one day," she tried again.

"Imagine I will."

Maddy nodded slowly, let the words sink in, and for the first time the finality of this situation truly hit.

The moment she'd stepped off the plane, she'd begun counting the seconds until she could flee this desolate place. But when she left she would also be leaving Beau behind, her best friend's beautiful gift to the world. When, if ever, would she see Beau again? There must be occasions when Jack flew to Sydney. Perhaps he could bring Beau, too.

Maddy was busy planning when they rounded the side of the homestead. A woman was moving down the wide front steps, winding her hands over a white apron, which was tied at the nape as well as around her ample girth. Her glossy hair was cropped short, polished jet threaded with silver. Soft lids hung over inquisitive cappuccino eyes, and as she rolled down each step, Maddy's nose picked up the mouth-watering smell of scones fresh from the oven.

Negotiating the last step, the woman extended both her hand and a cheery grin. Maddy smiled at the dab of flour on the woman's cheek and the aura of hominess and good humor she gave off.

"You must be Madison." The woman's grip was firm though not at all challenging. "I'm Cait." She nodded heartily, wiping her free hand down the apron. "Welcome to Leadeebrook."

"Jack's told me all about you."

Not exactly true. He'd provided minimal detail and only after some solid pressing. Cait Yolsen had been Leadeebrook's housekeeper for ten years. She was a widow with two children and two grown grandchildren. Maddy had been there when Jack had rung Cait to let her know to expect visitors. Afterward he'd relayed that Cait's cooking was exceptional. Maddy could taste those buttery scones now.

Cait moved close to Jack and the baby. Maddy's heart dissolved as Beau peered up at the stranger, eyes wide and intelligent, while he lay nestled in the crook of his uncle's arm.

Work-worn hands went to Cait's mouth as a hiccup of emotion escaped. "Oh, my, my, my." A tender smile glistened in her eyes. "Isn't he the handsome one." Her gaze darted to Maddy. "Did he sleep the whole way?"

"He was an angel—" Maddy turned to Jack "—wasn't he?"

Jack made a noise of affirmation, but the ghost of an approving smile lifted one corner of his mouth. *No colicky kid here.*

"He'll need a diaper change," said Cait.

"Absolutely," agreed Maddy.

Then they said together, "I'll take him."

But Jack rotated the baby away from two sets of eager hands.

Above those mirror glasses, his brow wrinkled. "Do I look helpless?"

Maddy blinked. "You want to *change* him?" In response, one wry dark brow rose. She rephrased. "I mean, don't you want a lesson or something first?"

"I've shorn over two hundred sheep in a single working day." He sidled past the women and up the steps. "I think I can shake a little talc and do up a couple of pins."

There *were* no pins; Dahlia had put Beau in disposables. That was what filled one of her big bags back on the plane. But Maddy held her tongue. If Jack wanted to assume the reins straight away—if he needed to dive in to prove himself—who was she to argue?

The man could shear two hundred sheep in one day.

At the top of the steps, Maddy noticed Nell, her dark eyes super-glued on Jack's every movement.

"You must be parched," Cait was saying as she ascended the steps, too.

When Nell padded into the homestead after Jack, Maddy followed the housekeeper. "I am a little dry."

"How's a cup of tea sound?"

"I'd prefer something cold, if you have it."

Still climbing, Cait gave a knowing, wistful sigh. "My husband was a stockman. We dated for two weeks and next I knew we were shacked up, working in the Northern Territory. Rugged land. Crocodiles, you know. Never thought I'd get used to the heat and the bull dust and the flies." The corners of her mouth swept up. "But you do."

Maddy blew at the hair clinging to her forehead. "I won't be here long enough to find out."

She had a career back in Sydney...friends...an exciting

full life. Needing to say goodbye to Beau until she saw him again would hurt terribly—she slapped another fly—but she already knew she wouldn't miss this place.

Halfway up, Cait stopped and touched the younger woman's hand. "I was sorry to hear about poor Dahlia. You must have been fast friends to help her out this way."

Maddy remembered how she'd made it through the chapel service yesterday with Beau asleep in her arms and a run of tears slipping quietly down her cheeks. Whenever the raw ache of emotion had threatened to break free, she'd concentrated on the pastor's calming words and the soft light filtering in through serene lofty windows.

Jack had sat beside her in the front left-hand pew. In an impeccable black suit, the set of his shoulders hadn't slipped once. Dahlia's university friends had recited prayers, poems or anecdotes, but her brother had kept his lidded gold-flecked eyes trained dead ahead.

Funneling down a breath, Maddy brought herself back and nodded. "Dahlia was the best friend I ever had."

Never too busy to listen. Never judgmental or rude. She was the easiest-going person Maddy had ever met. Which begged the question: how had two siblings with the same parents ended up with such different natures? Jack must be the most ornery person south of the equator.

Cait resumed her climb. "The bairn is lucky to have you."

Maddy smiled. Bairn as in baby.

"Dahlia wanted Jack to raise him," she explained. "I promised I'd help with the transition."

Cait dropped her gaze. "I'm sure she knew what she was doing."

Maddy's step faltered. Cait had reservations about Jack's suitability as a guardian, too? Dahlia hadn't got along with Jack; Maddy felt certain she, herself, would never penetrate his armor. Nell, on the other hand, idolized him. But Nell was a dog.

How had Jack treated his wife?

A curse blasted out of a nearby window and both women jumped. Maddy's palm pressed against her stomach. *Jack.* Was he having trouble opening the talc bottle?

Nausea crept up the back of her throat.

Oh Lord, had he dropped the baby?

Cait bolted, flinging open the front screen door, and when she sped into a room to the right, Maddy quickly followed. Her gaze landed on the baby, lying bare-bottomed on his back on a changing table, which was set up against a side wall. Jack stood before the table, his posture hunched, hands out, fingers spread, his expression darker than usual. He was gaping at a wet patch on his shirt while Beau kicked his feet and cooed. A bemused Nell was backed up in the corner, her head angled to one side.

When Jack had taken off the diaper, the baby must have squirted him.

Maddy cupped her mouth to catch the laugh. Why were the strongest men sometimes the biggest babies?

Struggling to compose herself, she sauntered forward. "I see you had a waterworks accident."

"*I* wasn't the one who had the accident." He touched the wet patch then flicked his hand. "At least he's a good aim."

Cait's chuckle came from behind. "I'll leave you both to do damage control," she said then asked about the baby's formula. Maddy handed her a bottle and can from a separate segment of Beau's bag. Cait called, "C'mon, Nell." The dog skulked out the doorway behind the housekeeper and Maddy gave a sigh of relief.

When Beau was cleaned up and in a fresh diaper,

Maddy slipped him carefully up and nuzzled her lips against his satin soft brow.

"I'm amazed he didn't freak out when you yelled like that," she said, rubbing the baby's back the way he liked. "I thought you might've dropped him."

When Maddy pivoted around, her mind froze solid while her response systems went into overload. His frown deep, Jack was grumbling, wrestling out of that soiled shirt.

Bronzed. Breathtakingly broad.

The walls seemed to darken and drag away at the same time the breath left her lungs and a sizzling, marvelous current swept through her body. Maddy unconsciously licked her lips.

Jack Prescott's chest was better than any she'd seen, airbrushed billboards included. His shoulders were sculpted from polished oak, his biceps were naturally, beautifully pumped, and the knockout expanse in between was dusted with the quintessential amount of coal black hair. She knew his flesh would be hot to the touch. Knew the landscape would be bedrock hard.

Maddy's gaze dropped.

And if that was the *top* half…

Cursing under his breath, Jack tore the sleeves from his arms and dumped the damp shirt at his feet.

He'd helped birth lambs more times than he could count. In comparison, this was child's play—literally. Being hosed by a baby wasn't a big deal. Three years ago he'd have done anything to have experienced just this kind of scene…to have been given the chance to care for his own little boy.

Raw emotion torqued in his chest. But he beat the pain

down before black memories took over. Feeling nothing was better than feeling angry.

Feeling helpless.

When he glanced up from the shirt, Maddy was standing stock still, jaw hanging. Holding Beau tight, she was staring at everything between his neck and his navel. Then her gaze dropped lower. Taken off guard—*again*—his muscles contracted as a coil of dark arousal snaked up his legs.

Inhaling, Jack set his jaw.

He'd already acknowledged his feelings for Madison Tyler. She was a looker, obviously intelligent. She also had guts. When Jack Prescott drew his pistols, most people had the good sense to run, but back in Sydney she'd stood her ground. She'd insisted she do right by his sister. He admired her for that. Frankly, his curiosity was piqued by the whole package.

But this physical attraction was headed nowhere. He was as good as engaged. Practically set to marry. Even if he *were* free, this woman wasn't what he needed. And vice versa. Clearly she was not the least impressed by what he held most dear—this rugged, sprawling land. Hell, she didn't even like *horses* whereas Tara was the only female he knew who could give him a run for his money galloping full bore down a straight.

So why was his gaze pinned to this woman's legs?

A growl of appreciation rumbled in his chest.

Because they were shapely, *that's* why. Long and milk white, and his fingers itched to know if they were as fine and silky smooth as they looked.

The baby squeaked and Jack came back to earth with a jolt. Shoving a hand through his hair, he shifted the thickness from his throat. He had no business indulging those images, particularly the vision of his houseguest in a negligee…the filmy, sultry kind that might wave and swirl around her slim ankles on a breezy summer night.

When heavy footfalls sounded down the timber floors of the hall, the full quota of Jack's senses came reeling back. Needing a distraction, he swiped his shirt off the floor and wadded it up while Maddy, seemingly needing a distraction, too, spun back to the changing table, busying herself with the baby's bag.

Jack had assumed a cool mask by the time Cait appeared and chimed, "Bottle's ready. I'd be happy to give him his feeding. It's been a long while." Cait extended her arms and Beau put out one of his. Sighing happily, she took and jiggled the wide-eyed baby. "Seems I haven't lost the touch." Then her attention skated over to his state of undress and her lips twitched. "Can I get you a fresh shirt, Jack?"

He held the wadded shirt higher and replied in a low, even voice. "S'right. I'll get one."

On her way out, the housekeeper tossed over one shoulder, "There's a pot of tea on the back veranda and a cool pitcher, too."

Maddy thanked Cait, flicked him an anxious glance, then, for something more to do, performed a fidgety finger comb of her flaxen hair behind each ear.

The entire "checking each other out" episode had lasted no more than a few seconds. They were a man and a woman who'd experienced a moment where natural attraction and physical impulse had temporarily taken over.

Jack drew up tall.

It wouldn't happen again. He hadn't brought city girl Madison Tyler here to seduce her. She was on his property only for the baby's sake. He owed that to his sister. But in two weeks, Maddy would be gone from Leadeebrook. Gone and out of his life. No use getting tangled up in it.

He headed for the door and didn't stop when her voice came from behind.

"Cait'll be a big help with Beau," she said, conversationally.

"She'll take good care of him."

"So you won't be hiring a nanny?"

"Won't need one."

Tara wanted a family. Now, ready or not, they had one. But there was time enough to tell Maddy about Beau's future stepmother. Time enough to let Tara know she was about to become an instant parent. After the news sank in, he couldn't imagine Tara would be anything other than pleased. But that wasn't the kind of information one shared over the phone. He'd tell her in person, in private.

Tomorrow was soon enough.

As he sauntered down the hall, Jack felt Maddy's gaze burning a hole in his back. Not meeting her eyes, he jerked a thumb toward his bedroom doorway.

"I'll grab a shirt and we'll get to that pot of tea."

A moment later he stood in front of his wardrobe, retrieving a button-down from its hanger. Out of the corner of his eye he spied movement—probably Nellie-girl keeping tabs on things. But when he checked, it was Maddy who hovered in the doorway, and this time her gaze wasn't fused on him. Her attention was riveted on the chest of drawers to her immediate right. On the photo he kept there and never put away.

Her face visibly pale, her round gaze hovered over to his.

"I—I'm sorry," she stammered. "I had no idea. I thought you must be going to the laundry. I thought the main bedroom would be upstairs."

Jaw tight, he drove his arms through the sleeves then, leaving buttons undone and tails hanging. He took her arm and ushered her out into the hall. Did she have to follow him around like a newborn calf? Was she purposely trying to get in the way and whip up his blood?

Once in the hall, he released his hold and told himself that would be thc *last* time he'd feel her skin on his. If looking was bad, touching was a million times worse. Or was that a million times better?

Growling, he shook that unwelcome thought from his brain and headed toward the veranda, purposefully fastening each shirt button, then rolling the sleeves to the elbow. "Cait'll have set the tray out here."

Out on the veranda, he fell into a chair, lifted the food net and nodded at the spread of scones and cupcakes. After she accepted a scone, he grabbed a cake. He chomped off a mouthful and chewed, studying the plains and daring her to ask the question that must be tingling on the tip of her tongue. He could hear the words rattling around in her head.

The lady in the photo...was she your wife?

But Maddy didn't ask. Rather she sat quietly on the other side of the small square table, her chair backed up against the wall, as was his. She poured one glass of lemonade and one cup of tea and passed it over.

After a tense moment, he flicked her a sidelong glance. She was sipping her drink, surveying his favorite stretch of land—the dip between what was known on the property as Twelve Gum Ridge and Black Shore Creek. The knot binding the muscles between his shoulder blades eased fractionally. A moment more and he crossed an ankle over the opposite knee.

As three full-grown red kangaroos bounded across the shimmering horizon, Maddy sighed.

"I can't get over the quiet." She craned her neck, trying to see farther. "Where do you keep the sheep?"

He uncrossed his ankle and sat straighter. "Don't have any."

She tossed him a look. "Sorry. I thought you said you don't have any sheep."

"I got rid of them...three years ago."

She blinked several times then offered a nod as if she understood. But she didn't. Unless you'd lived the nightmare, no one could understand what it meant to lose both your wife and your child in one day. The world had looked black after that. As black and charred as his heart had been. He hadn't cared about sheep or money.

About anything.

"What do you do on a sheep station with no sheep?" she asked after a time. "Don't you get bored?"

He set down his cup and said what should have been obvious. "Leadeebrook is my home."

Urban folk weren't programmed to appreciate what the land had to offer. The freedom to think. The room to simply be. As much as his father had tried to convert her, his mother had never fully appreciated it either.

Besides, there was plenty of maintenance to keep a man busy if he went looking for it.

He dumped sugar into his cup. "It's a different way of living out here. A lot different from the city."

"A *lot*."

"No smog."

"No people."

"Just the way I like it."

"Don't you miss civilization?"

His face deadpanned. "Oh, I prefer being a barbarian."

She pursed her lips, considering. "That's a strong word, but in a pinch..."

He had every intention of staring her down, but a different emotion rose up and he grinned instead. They might not see eye to eye, but she was...amusing.

Seeing his grin, a smile lit her eyes and she sat back more. "How many acres do you have?"

"Now, just under five thousand. Back in its heyday, Leadeebrook was spread over three hundred thousand acres and carried two hundred thousand sheep, but after World War II land was needed for war service and agricultural settlement so my great-grandfather and grandfather decided to sell off plots to soldier settlers. The soil here is fertile. Their forward planning helped make an easier transition from grazing to farming. That industry's the mainstay of this district now. Keeps people employed."

"I take it back." Her voice carried a sincere note of respect. "You're not a barbarian."

"Save your opinion until after you've eaten my brown snake on an open spit."

She chuckled. "You do have a sense of humor." Her smile withered. "You are joking, right?"

He only spooned more sugar into his tea.

One leg crooked up under the other as she turned toward him. "Did you have a happy childhood growing up here?"

"Couldn't have asked for a better one. My family was wealthy. Probably far wealthier than most people even realized. But we lived a relatively simple life, with some good old-fashioned hard work thrown in for good measure."

"Where did you go to school?"

"Went to the town first off then boarding school in

Sydney. I came home every vacation. I'd help with dipping, shearing, lambing and tagging."

Her smile wistful, she laid her elbow on the table between them and cupped her jaw in her palm. "You make it sound almost romantic."

Almost?

He forced his gaze away from her mouth and let it settle on the picturesque horizon.

"Have you ever seen a sunset like that? I sit out here, lapping up those colors, and know this is how God intended for us to live. Not rushing around like maniacs on multilane freeways, chained to a computer fourteen hours a day. This is paradise."

Sue had thought the same way.

They sat saying nothing, simply looking at the rose-gold pallet darken against a distant smudge of hills. Most nights he took in the dusk, soaking in the sense of connectedness it gave. Sometimes, for a few moments, he felt half at peace.

"Will you ever stock up again?" she asked after a time.

He had plenty invested in bonds and real estate around the country. Despite the wool industry having seen better days, he was more comfortable financially than any of his ancestors, and had harbored dreams of reshaping Leadeebrook to its former glory. He and Sue used to discuss their ideas into the night, particularly during the last stages of her pregnancy. There'd been so much to look forward to and build on together. Now…

His stomach muscles double-clutched and he set his cup aside.

Now he was responsible for Dahlia's boy. He would give the lad every opportunity. Would care for him like a father. But that feeling…?

He swallowed against the stone in his throat.

He wished he could be the man he'd once been. But when his family died, that man had died, too.

"No," he said, his gaze returning to the sunset. "I'll never stock up again."

She was asking another question but his focus had shifted to a far off rumbling—thc distant groan of a motor. He knew the vehicle. Knew the driver.

Lord and Holy Father.

He unfolded to his feet and groaned.

He wasn't ready for this meeting yet.

Four

The white Land Cruiser skidded to a stop a few feet from a nearby water tank, dry grass spewing out in dusty clouds from behind its monster wheels. A woman leaped out and, without shutting the driver's door, sailed up the back steps.

Maddy clutched her chair's arms while her gaze hunted down Jack.

He'd heard the engine before she had. Had pushed up and now came to a stop by the veranda rail, his weight shifted to one side so that the back pockets of his jeans and those big shoulders lay slightly askew. When the woman reached him, no words were exchanged. She merely bounced up on tiptoe, flung her arms around his neck and, her cheek to his, held on.

Maddy pressed back into the early evening shadows. This scene was obviously meant for two. Who was this woman? If she wasn't Jack Prescott's lover, she sure as rain wanted to be.

Maddy's gaze tracked downward.

The woman's riding boots—clean and expensive by the emblem—covered her fitted breeches to the knee. She was slender and toned; with a mane of ebony hair, loose and lush, she might have been the human equivalent of a prized thoroughbred. Her olive complexion hinted at Mediterranean descent and her onyx eyes were filled with affection as she drew back and peered up into Jack's—passionate and loyal.

Maddy's mouth pulled to one side.

Seemed Jack had indeed moved on since the death of his wife—the auburn-haired woman whose photo she'd seen on that chest of drawers. When they'd come face to face earlier in the nursery and she'd copped an eye full of Jack's all-male-and-then-some chest, she'd imagined he'd felt the moment, too. She'd told herself that's why he'd been particularly brusque afterward. The lightning bolt—the overwhelming awareness—had struck him, as well, and, taken aback, he hadn't known how to handle it.

But clearly that fiery, unexpected reaction had been one-sided. He'd seemed vexed by the scene in the nursery because he was embarrassed over her ogling. Embarrassed and annoyed. He was spoken for, and this woman in front of her might capture and hold any man, even I-am-an-island Jack Prescott.

With a fond but strained smile, Jack unfastened the woman's hold and her palms slid several inches down from his thick neck to his shirt. She toyed with a button as she gazed adoringly into his eyes and sighed.

"You're home." Then she tilted her head, that ebony mane spilled over her shoulder and her smile became a look of mild admonition. "I wish you'd have let me come to Sydney with you. It must have been so hard facing the funeral on your own. I shouldn't have promised that I'd stay behind."

Jack found her hand on his chest and carefully brought it to her side. "Tara, I brought somebody back with me."

The woman slowly straightened, blinked. Then, having dialed into her personal radar, she honed in on Maddy. The woman's thickly lashed eyes darkened more while her complexion dropped a shade. As their gazes locked, Tara surreptitiously found and held the veranda rail at her back.

Maddy's face flushed hot. She knew what this woman, Tara, was thinking. The accusation blazed in her eyes. But she and Jack were not an item. They weren't even friends, and from the venom building in this woman's eyes, the sooner she knew all the facts the better.

Maddy found her feet at the same time Jack beckoned her over.

"This is Madison Tyler," he said, then nodded to the woman. "Tara Anderson."

An uneven smile broke across Tara's face. "Madison. We haven't met before—" her eyes narrowed slightly "—have we?"

Jack stepped in. "Maddy's staying at Leadeebrook for a couple of weeks."

"Oh?" Tara's practiced smile almost quivered. "Why?"

Before anyone could answer, Cait appeared at the back doorway, holding Beau. The housekeeper's jovial expression slid when she recognized their visitor.

"Tara, love. I heard the truck. I thought it was Snow."

Tara's hand slipped off the rail and when her startled, glistening gaze slid from the baby to Jack, Maddy's heart sank in her chest. Tara's thoughts were as loud as war drums. She thought the child belonged to them—to her and Jack. Yet everything in Tara Anderson's stunned expression said she couldn't let herself believe the worst. She wanted to trust the man she so obviously cared for.

As if afraid he might vanish, Tara tentatively touched Jack's hand and her voice cracked when she asked, "Jack…?"

"This is Dahlia's son," he said in a somber tone. "The father isn't on the scene. Maddy was Dahlia's friend. She promised my sister she'd help the baby settle in here."

Drawing back, Tara audibly exhaled, then touched her brow with an unsteady hand. She shook her head as if to dispel a fog but her expression remained pained.

"Dahlia's son…" She breathed out again before her gaze pierced his. "You agreed to this, Jack? To a *baby?* I thought you said—"

His brows tipped together. "We won't discuss it now."

"When *were* we going to discuss it?" she asked. "How long have you known?"

But the line of his mouth remained firm. Turning, he set his hands on the rail and peered out over the barren landscape.

The anxiety in Maddy's stomach balled tighter. Hearing that Jack was responsible for a baby had been a massive shock for Tara Anderson; she wanted answers. Without knowing their history, Maddy couldn't help but think she deserved them. And yet Jack kept his shoulders set and his gaze fixed on something in the distance. He could be so bloody stubborn sometimes.

It wasn't her place to interfere, but if she could ease the tension a little by extending the hand of friendship, Maddy decided she would. If Jack and this woman were as close as this scene suggested, Beau would be seeing more of Tara…more than he would see of his aunt Maddy.

She edged closer. “Do you live in town, Tara?”

Tara’s bewildered gaze whipped around, as if she’d forgotten they had company.

“I own the adjoining property,” she said absently. Then a different emotion filtered over her face and she exhaled once more, this time with an apologetic smile. “Forgive me, please. I’m being rude. It’s just…” She sought out Jack’s gaze. “I’ve been worried these past days.”

“Will you stay for supper?” Cait asked from the back door, giving Beau, who had half his fist in his mouth, a jiggle. “There’s always plenty.”

At the same time Tara quizzed Jack’s face for his reaction, Maddy felt a brush against her leg. She lowered her gaze. Nell had taken up a seat between herself and Jack.

Stiffening, Maddy rubbed the goosebumps from her arm and slid a foot away. A mime act made more noise than this dog.

When Jack rotated away from the rail to face Tara, the familiar furrow between his brows was gone. Accommodating now, he reached for her hand. “Yes, of course. Stay for supper.”

But Tara stole a quick glance between the baby and Maddy then, put on a lighthearted air and shook back her ebony hair.

“I would’ve liked to, but I’m staying in town tonight. Taking a buyer to dinner.”

Jack eased back against the rail and crossed his arms over his chest, interested. “Which horse?”

“Hendrix.” She addressed Maddy. “I breed Warmbloods.”

Maddy raised her brows. And she was supposed to know what that meant? But she imitated Jack’s cross-armed stance, pretending to be interested, too.

"That's…great."

"Warmbloods are bred for equestrian sports," Jack explained. "Tara's trained a stable full of champions, mainly Hanoverians."

Maddy tacked up her slipping smile. If she'd felt inadequate before…

No wonder Jack was involved with this woman. Beautiful, ultimately gracious under pressure, and a proven breeder of champions to boot. What more could a man want?

With an elegant, slightly possessive air, Tara looped her arm through Jack's. "Will you walk me down to the car?"

As Jack pushed off the rail, Maddy piped up, "If I don't see you before I head back to Sydney, it was nice meeting you."

Tara's lips tightened even as they stretched into a charming smile. "Oh, you'll see me."

As she and Jack meandered down the steps, Maddy couldn't help but notice—Tara didn't say goodbye to Beau.

Later that evening, Maddy went to join Jack in the yard. With his back to her, he didn't seem to hear her approach, so she cleared her throat and asked, "Don't suppose you want any company?"

When Jack turned his head—his eyes glittering in the evening shadows, his face devoid of emotion—Maddy drew back and withered in her shoes. She shouldn't have left the house and come outside. Standing amidst the cricket-clicking tranquility, it was clear Jack didn't want company. Particularly not hers.

After that awkward scene three hours ago with Tara Anderson, Jack had taken a vehicle out to the hangar to bring the bags in. Then he'd mumbled something about heading off for a while. From the window of her guest bedroom, Maddy had caught sight of a big black horse cantering away. With an Akubra slanted low on his brow, the rider looked as if he'd been born to rule from the saddle.

As he headed off toward the huge molten ball sinking into the hills, her chest had squeezed. She might have been watching a scene from a classic Western movie. Talk about larger than life.

While Cait prepared dinner, Maddy had enjoyed a quick shower. Then it was Beau's turn. He'd splashed and squealed in his bath until she had a stitch in her side from laughing and the front of her dress was soaked through. She didn't want to dwell on the fact that someone else would be enjoying this time with Beau soon.

Would that someone be Tara?

She neither saw nor heard Jack return, but when Cait called dinner, as if by magic he appeared in the meals room. With his gaze hooded and broad shoulders back, he'd promptly pulled out a chair for her at the table. She'd grinned to herself. Jack might be a lot of things, but Beau would learn his manners in this house.

The baked meal smelled divine, but Jack's masculine just-showered scent easily trumped it. His wet hair, slicked back off his brow, was long enough to lick the back of his white collar. He'd shaved, too, although the shadow on his jaw was a permanent feature...an enduring sexy sandpaper smudge.

When the baby was settled in the playpen beside the table, Jack had threaded his hands, bowed his head and said a brief but touching grace about missing loved ones and taking new ones into their home. Maddy had swallowed against the sudden lump in her throat. There was a deeper, more yielding side to this seemingly impenetrable man. There *must* be. In that moment, Maddy regretted she wouldn't come to know it.

As they sat down to dinner, Cait told Maddy of Leadeebrook's main dining room, with its long, grand table and crystal chandelier set in the center of a high, molded ceiling. But that room was kept for special occasions. She and Jack mainly ate here, in the meals area off the kitchen. After promising to show Maddy around the house the next day, Cait flicked out her linen napkin and asked to hear all the news from the city.

Jack didn't seem to care either way. The gold flecks gone from his eyes, he seemed more distracted than ever. While he cut and forked his way through the meal, the ladies chatted, watching over the baby who played with his bunch-of-keys rattle.

When Beau began to grumble, Maddy left to put him down. After firmly taking charge earlier, she was interested that Jack didn't say boo about helping with Beau's first bedtime in his new home. Maybe the memory of that wet shirt still haunted him, but Maddy suspected thoughts of Tara and her reaction to his guardianship of the baby weighed heavily on Jack's mind tonight. How would he handle the divide?

Beau had drifted off without a whimper. After laying a light sheet over his tiny sleeping form, she tiptoed back into the kitchen. That's when Cait had suggested she join Jack outside here in the cool.

Maddy had grown warm all over at the thought, which only proved that being alone with Jack under the expansive Southern Cross sky was not a good idea. But she'd made the effort. She didn't want to provoke any fires—physical or anything else—but neither could she afford to leave here, for the most part, a stranger. Jack had to know that if he needed her, for Beau's sake, despite any personal hiccups, she would always be there. Dahlia would've wanted that, and Maddy wanted that, too.

She and Jack needed to be able to communicate, at least on some level.

She'd found him here, one shoulder propped up against an ancient-looking tree, while he rubbed a rag over a bridle.

"Is the baby down?" he asked.

With nerves jittering in her stomach, she nodded and inched closer. "Now he's down, he shouldn't wake up till around seven."

Stopping at his side, she joined him in taking in a view of the hushed starry sky while that rag worked methodically over the steel bit. A horse's whinny carried on a fresh breeze. A frog's lonely croak echoed nearby. And Jack kept polishing.

If anyone was going to start a conversation, it'd have to be her.

She shifted her weight. "How long have you had the black horse?"

"From a colt."

"Bet he was glad to see you back."

"Not as glad as I was to see him."

She raised her brows. Well, a cowboy's best friend was supposed to be his horse.

She leaned against another nearby tree, her hands laced behind the small of her back. "Where did you ride off to earlier?"

"I needed to catch up with Snow Gibson. He lives in the caretaker's cabin a couple miles out."

Maddy recalled an earlier conversation. "Cait said Snow's quite a character."

A hint of a smile hooked his mouth and they both

fell into silence again…tangible and yet not entirely uncomfortable. Guess there was something to be said for the advantages of this untainted country air.

Giving into a whim, she shut her eyes, tilted her face to the stars and let more than the subtle breeze whisper to her senses. She imagined she felt that magnetism rippling off Jack Prescott in a series of heatwaves and her own aura glowing and transforming in response. She imagined the way his slightly roughened hands might feel sliding over her skin…sensual, stirring. Enthralling.

Opening her eyes, willing away the awareness, she shut off those dangerous thoughts and focused on a heavy star hanging low on the horizon. She wasn't here to indulge in fantasies, no matter how sweet or how strong. She was here to do a job and get back to where she belonged.

Besides, Jack's affections were spoken for. Tara had made her position on that clear: *Hands off.*

Suddenly weary, Maddy pushed off the tree.

She shouldn't have come out here. Talking with Jack was like trying to push an elephant up a hill. She needed to accept this situation for what it was. She needed to chill out and let things between herself and Jack unravel naturally. Right now, she needed to say good-night.

She was about to take her leave when Jack's deep graveled voice drifted through the night.

"This property's been in my family since 1869." He angled his head toward a long stationary shadow to their left. "See that trough?"

He began to walk. Maddy threw a look at the back door then inwardly shrugged. Slapping the impression of bark from her palms, she followed. If he was making an effort, she would, too.

"This trough was a wedding gift," Jack was saying. "My great-great grandfather suggested to his wife he should cut a hole in the bathroom wall and they could use it as a tub as well as to water the horses in the yard."

Maddy blanched. She had a feeling he was serious. *Thank heaven for modern-day plumbing. How had women survived out here back then?*

"I carved my initials here when I was six," he went on and swept one long tanned finger over an etching in the wood. "Our dog had just had pups." He pointed to several nicks—One, two, three… Seven pups. He straightened and, studying her, weighed the bridle in his hand. "You never had a dog?"

"I had piano lessons and lots of dresses."

"But no dog," he persisted.

"No dog."

Something rustled in the brush nearby at the same time he lifted and dropped one shoulder. "You missed out."

Focused on the brush—was it a snake, a dingo?—she admitted, "I was attacked by a Doberman cross when I was young."

His expression froze before he blindly set the bridle down on the trough. "Maddy…God, I'm sorry."

Weeks spent in hospital, years of fighting the phobia. She made herself shrug. "Could've been worse."

He held her gaze for several heartbeats then slipped her a wry smile. "I got the shakes once. I broke my arm jumping a stallion over a creek when I was ten. He was the most cantankerous horse I've ever known."

Maddy openly grinned. Quite the confession coming from Crocodile Dundee.

He walked again, a meandering comfortable gait that invited her to join him.

"Piano and dresses," he murmured. "So you were a mummy's girl."

"My mother died when I was five."

His step faltered. She almost saw the shudder pass through his body. "Wait a minute. I need to take that other foot out of my mouth."

She wasn't offended. He couldn't have known.

"I have one perfect memory of her tucking me into bed. She had a beautiful smile." Her favorite photo she kept in her wallet—a candid shot of her mother laughing and holding her first and only baby high against a clear blue day.

"Your dad still around?"

The snapshot in Maddy's mind faded and she squared her shoulders. "Uh-huh. He's great. Really energized. I work for him at Tyler Advertising."

"I've heard of it. Well-respected firm." He kicked a rock with the toe of his boot. "So you're a chip off the ol' block?"

"Hopefully. I have my first big deal coming together soon."

"In for a big bonus?"

"I guess."

In the moonlight, his lidded gaze assessed her. "But that's not your motivation."

"Not at all."

"You want to make your father proud," he surmised and she nodded.

"That's not so unusual. Besides I really like the industry," she added. "Lots of exciting people and events. It's where I belong."

She believed that and finally her father was believing it, too. She'd seen the look in his eyes when she'd told him at sixteen she wanted to be an account executive with the firm; he didn't think she had it in her. He'd said the words, *You're more like your mother,* which meant she wasn't strong enough. Her mother had been a gentle person and, no, she hadn't been able to beat the leukemia, but she and her mother were two separate issues, two separate people. And once she had the client's signature on the bottom line…

"You must be chomping at the bit to get back," Jack said, coming to stand beside a weathered post and rail fence.

Her lips twitched. "I won't deny I'll be happy to leave the flies behind."

"They don't eat much. It's the bull ants you have to worry about."

"So I'd better not stand in one spot for too long."

He chuckled—a rich easy sound that fit him as well as those delectable jeans. She couldn't think of another man with more sex appeal…the energy he expelled was as formidable and natural as thunder on a stormy night. On the *What Makes a Man Maddeningly Irresistible* list, Jack got double ticks in every box.

When she realized their shared look had lasted longer than it ought to, a blush bloomed over her cheeks. As the heat spread to her breasts and belly, Jack rubbed the back of his neck and moved off again.

"How did you meet Dahlia?"

"A university friend," she said, willing the husky quality from her voice. "Dahlia was a couple of years younger than me. We were enrolled in different majors, but we met at a party and hit it off. She had the best laugh. Infectious." *Kind of like yours,* she wanted to say, *only not so deep.*

Looking off, he scrubbed his temple with a knuckle. "Yeah. I remember her laugh."

Maddy stayed the impulse to touch his arm—to offer some show of comfort. Men like Jack were all about strength, intelligence and making decisions. Jack was a leader and leaders didn't dilute their power with displays of emotion, either given or received. In an emergency, he would act and act well. Even standing in the uneventful quiet of this night, Maddy found a sense of reassurance in knowing that. Some silly part of her almost wanted to admit it out loud.

Instead she said, "You must have missed that sound when she left here."

A muscle ticked a strong beat in his jaw and he let out a long breath. "My wife begged me to go after her but I was determined not to. Some sorry home truths came out that last night. I figured if Dahlia wanted to find her own way, I wouldn't stop her."

But his tone said he regretted it.

"She didn't like Leadeebrook?"

"She liked it okay," he said, crossing his arms as he strolled, "but she didn't feel the same way I feel. The way my father felt, too. She didn't want to stay here, 'shrivel up and die,' as she put it. She'd said she'd had enough of station existence to last a lifetime."

Which would have cut her brother's loyal Prescott heart in two.

"And your wife…how did she feel about the station?"

He searched the sky as if she might be listening and looking down, and Maddy knew in that moment that he'd loved his wife very much.

"This was Sue's home. Always will be." His thoughtful expression sharpened then, frowning, he angled toward the house. "Was that the baby?"

Maddy listened then shook her head. "I didn't hear anything. Cait said she'd keep an ear out." They walked again, toward a timber structure she thought was the stables. When next she spoke, Maddy put a lighter note in her tone.

"Tara Anderson is obviously a big fan of the land, too."

His gaze caught hers and as his look intensified, Maddy's skin flared with a pleasant, telling warmth. The way he was looking at her now, she could almost fool herself into believing that she, not Tara, was the woman with whom he was involved...that the primal heat smoldering in his eyes was meant for her and her only.

When a different, more guarded light rose up in his eyes and he broke the gaze, Maddy's shoulders dropped and she told her pulse to slow down. Dynamic in every sense of the word, he was more of a man than any she'd known. That was the reason she imagined heat waves rippling off him and wrapping themselves around her. Not because this moonlight was affecting him as it was clearly affecting her.

"Tara and I have known each other a long while," he said. "Her uncle and my father were friends. Sue and Tara became good friends, too. They shared similar values, similar interests. So do we."

"Are you going to marry her?"

A red-hot bolt dropped through her middle at the same time her eyes grew to saucers and she swallowed a gulping breath. Had she actually said that? Yes, she'd been wondering—a lot. But to *ask*...

She held up both hands. "I'm sorry. That is so none of my business."

Beneath the star-strewn sky, Jack's gaze held hers for a protracted moment. Then he set his hands low on his belt and tracked his narrowed gaze over to the distant peaks of the Great Dividing Range.

He nodded. "There's been talk of it."

Maddy let out that breath. So Tara had good reason to be so demonstrative this afternoon. She saw Jack as her future husband. A husband who'd gone to a funeral and had brought back a baby.

Maddy chewed her lip. She shouldn't ask—she might not like the answer—but she couldn't keep the question down.

"Does Tara like children?"

He scratched the tip of his ear. "That's a sticking point. Tara wants a family very much..."

He'd been slow to accept responsibility for Beau. He approached his guardianship as a duty to be performed rather than a gift to be treasured. Now he was admitting that he didn't want a family.

Maddy knew one day she wanted be a mother. Caring for Beau had only heightened that knowledge. She couldn't imagine why any person wouldn't want to have their own family—to give and receive unconditional love. What had Jack's first wife to say about his aversion to fatherhood? More importantly, what did that admission mean for Beau?

She'd hoped, she'd prayed, but did Jack have what it took to be a good father to that baby? And there was Tara. She hadn't shown an interest in Beau other than out of shock and suspicion yet she wanted children of her own. If she and Jack married—if they had children together—would Tara see Beau as a nuisance or inconvenience when her own brood came along? If that were the case, what sort of family would poor Beau grow up in? What sort of damaged self-image would being an add-on leave him with?

A whinny sounded in the night and Maddy was brought back.

"Herc can hear us," Jack told her and jerked a thumb at the stables. "Want to meet him?"

Deep in thought, Maddy absently agreed but before

long the scent of horse and leather pulled her up. With a sneeze tickling her nose, she made an excuse.

"It's getting late. We probably shouldn't disturb him."

Jack laughed and kept walking. "Herc won't mind the company."

She pinched her nose. "I think I might be allergic."

That got his attention and he angled back around. "Have you been around horses before?"

"A real one?"

He grinned—a breathtaking, cheeky smile—and Maddy's breasts tingled with unbidden desire.

"You know, Maddy, there's nothing quite like the rhythm of a strong dependable horse rocking beneath you."

Rhythm…strong…rocking. Maddy blew out a breath. She wanted to fan herself. Did he have any clue how fiercely attractive he was?

"Thanks," she announced, dabbing her brow, "but I'll pass."

That smile widened and she imagined the fire in his eyes had licked her lips.

"Why not broaden your horizons? There's more to life than a wardrobe of pretty dresses."

"Or a stable of horses."

"You're right."

He sauntered over to stand, shoulder to shoulder, beside her as he checked out the trillion-star lightshow dancing over their heads. His innate energy—the physical pull she felt when he was this close—was as tangible as his body heat. She wished he hadn't moved nearer. And, dammit, she wished he'd moved nearer still.

"There's a cool breeze after a long muggy spell," he said, "and the dependability of a vast rich land like this. There's the satisfaction that comes with a hard day's work, and the lure of a full moon on a still night just like tonight. And then…"

His dark brows nudged together as if an odd idea had struck. When he turned his head, his expression had softened with an emotion she hadn't seen in him before. He blinked once then, as if he'd read all her earlier thoughts, he cupped her cheek and she stopped breathing.

"And then," he said, "there's this."

The pad of his thumb raised her chin and as his head dropped over hers, Maddy's faculties shut down. She might have wondered, might have dreamed, but having Jack Prescott's undivided smoldering attention focused only upon her had seemed beyond reason or possibility.

And yet now…

Maddy trembled, leaned in and pressed up.

With his mouth closed so perfectly over hers and his hard muscular frame pressed in tight all the world seemed to spiral away. With her heart beating high and hard, she couldn't think beyond the thrill of this moment, beyond the wonder of his fingertips working against her nape… the heavy throb low in her belly…and a fiery internal pulse that whispered to her about the promise of a slow, hot night spent in Jack Prescott's bed.

His thumb ran down her throat as he sipped and tasted and explored. When his mouth reluctantly left hers and her heavy eyelids opened, his eyes were smiling into hers. A delicious full-body quiver ran through her blood. She was light-headed, dizzy. Had Jack truly just kissed her? Had she truly kissed him back? On one level she couldn't digest the reality. The possibility that he would embrace her, gift her with the world's steamiest kiss, didn't compute. And yet as she stood now looking up into the shadowed perfection of his face, improbability faded into another understanding.

Her belly felt heavy with a need that acknowledged only deep physical desire. She wanted his mouth on hers again. With a longing she hadn't known she was capable of, she wanted his lips on her neck, on her breasts.

He stole another light, lingering kiss from the side of her mouth before his lips skimmed her jaw. "See what I mean about that full moon?"

His hand slid down her spine to circle the sensitive dip low in her back and the urge to coil her fingers up through his hair and mold herself against him became overpowering. Every labored breath compounded the desire building in her blood. Every thought confirmed that this felt way too good to let go.

How a bit of common sense survived the fire ripping through her veins, Maddy couldn't say. She didn't want to listen to reason. She only wanted to know his kiss again and again. And yet the danger...the *dishonesty* of this situation was as apparent as the aching desire. As much as she wanted to, she couldn't ignore the harm this kind of scene could and would do.

Finding her strength and her breath, she angled her head away. "This isn't right."

With a knuckle, he coaxed her mouth back to his. "This is *very* right."

When he drew her bottom lip into his mouth and the shaft behind his zipper flexed against her belly, her resolve slipped like hot wax spilling down a candle. The urge to give in was so sweet and so strong...but she couldn't ignore what was most important.

She pushed against his sturdy chest. "Jack, what about Tara?"

They needed to keep this complicated time as uncomplicated as they could. Yes, she was physically drawn to Jack—she'd like to meet a woman who wouldn't be. But a kiss would lead to more—to dark heady places she wasn't prepared to go. She wanted some kind of future with Beau. The last thing she needed was an ill-planned night hanging over her head and a stepmother who would then have good reason for suspicion.

He'd been so intense, so driven, she half expected him to ignore the obvious question. But he surprised her. Comprehension dawned in his eyes. His head pulled slowly back and his gaze searched hers as if he were coming out of a daze. When the horse whinnied again, he took a step away and his previously insistent palm left her back. His hand found the V at his opened collar and his gaze speared through her, as though he were seeing someone else.

His deep voice rumbled through the shadows.

"You should go inside."

A shiver chased up her spine. His face looked changed… almost vulnerable. Gingerly, she touched his strong hot arm but his intense expression didn't change.

He said again, "You should go."

Then he wove around her toward the stable.

Later, as she lay awake in bed staring at the ceiling, she heard the retreating beat of hooves. Still glowing from the feel of him, still buzzing from the high, she rolled over and lightly touched her lips.

She thought she'd been kissed before. Thought she knew what desire was…how it felt to be on fire.

She'd been wrong.

Five

The next morning, Jack drove into Hawksborough, a town that pretty much consisted of a main street lined with Leopard trees, a federation-style library, town hall and courthouse, and a series of fading shop fronts which led to the Shangri-la Motel.

Parked in front of Bruce's Barber's, a residence which co-let to Hawsborough's only bank, Jack swung out of the driver's side of his four-wheel drive and absorbed the town's aura of timelessness. Sue had loved this place almost as much as she'd loved the station. If he ever came in, Sue would, too, to catch up with the locals then veg out in the town square, working her way through one of her tomes. Sue had been as laid back as supper on Sundays.

Sophisticated Madison Tyler, on the other hand, fit in more with canapés and cocktails at five. She would find Hawksborough's sole set of traffic lights and single movie theater gauche. Possibly unsettling. Maddy cared about what happened to Dahlia's baby—he respected her for that—but as soon as her job here was done she'd be gone, back to the city and "civilization". Thirteen more days.

And nights.

As he removed his hat and crossed into the Shangri-la foyer, Jack knew he could fool himself and say he understood why he'd cast off proper conduct last night: he'd wanted to sample an intriguing wine, just a taste. He'd kissed Maddy. Had enjoyed the act immensely. Curiosity supposedly done and dusted. Trouble was, while all this rationalizing had been taking place, he'd forgotten about Tara. About the commitment he'd made to her. And that just wasn't him.

That Maddy was so different from Sue, from Tara—from any woman he'd known—might be a reason for his behavior but it wasn't an excuse. He felt off-center around her. Couldn't seem to shake her from his thoughts. At four this morning he'd finally figured out what needed to be done and how he should do it.

Now he strode up to Mrs. Claudia, the friendly gray-haired receptionist he'd known all his life. She slid the *Life* crossword to one side of the mahogany desk and they exchanged pleasantries about her aging canary and the lack of rain. Then he dialed up to the room Tara took whenever she stayed in town.

When she picked up on the second ring, Jack braced his shoulders. "Tara, I need to see you."

There was a moment's pause before a sigh came down the line. "Jack, it's you. Thank God. Come up."

From her thready tone, something wasn't right in her world. He could guess what. But as he set off for the vintage elevator, Jack knew he couldn't let any bad news delay his own.

When Tara opened her door, her hair was as glossy as

usual but her eyes didn't hold their normal fire. She lifted a large envelope and gave a jaded smile.

"Hendrix's X-rays. There's a small cyst on his hock. In my opinion, and the vet's, nothing to worry about." She flung the envelope on the TV stand. "But the buyer wants a cut in price."

"Three hundred G's is a lot for a horse," he said, hanging his hat on the hatstand.

"Not for a brilliant jumper." Then her dark eyes softened and an inviting smile curved her lips. "But let's not talk about that."

She took his hand and led him toward the bed. Jack kept his eyes straight ahead but even a blind man couldn't miss her attire: a short, pale pink silk wrap. From the outline, she was naked underneath.

She drew him toward the foot of the unmade bed. Positioning herself close, she wove her hands up his shirt front then, closing her eyes, she reached on tiptoe to rub her nose with his.

"It's so good to see you." Her fingers flexed in his shirt as she murmured, "Will I order up some breakfast?"

"I've eaten."

She opened her eyes at his tone and angled her head. "I need to apologize for the way I acted yesterday. But, you have to understand, I was taken aback. The last thing I expected to see was a baby—" she lowered to sit on the rumpled sheet "—or another woman." Twining her fingers with his, she urged him to sit beside her. "But I should've shown more control. You're right. We need to speak about this in private." She pivoted toward him, her wrap slipped but she didn't cover her thigh. "How do you feel about raising Dahlia's son?"

He set his jaw. "Committed."

"There is one big positive."

"You mean besides giving my nephew a home."

"Of course that baby deserves a home." Her touch filed over his thigh and settled on his leg. "And now there's no reason why *we* shouldn't start a family. I understand how you feel about losing your own. Jack, I can't imagine how much that must hurt, even now. But being given this baby is like being given another chance. We could give that little boy a brother or two." Her hand squeezed. "A real family, for us all."

He pushed to his feet and her hand fell away. "We need to talk."

"If you're worried about inheritance—that I might be biased toward the children we have together—I'm more than fine with all the children having equal shares..."

"I can't marry you."

She recoiled as if bitten by a snake. Her slender throat worked up and down as moisture welled in her eyes. His gut twisted around a heavy knot of guilt. There'd been no easy way to say it. But the admission had sounded blunt even to his ears.

"You can't marry..." She carefully unfolded to her feet. "We've discussed this. Gone through it." She stepped closer and a note of desperation lifted her voice. "What about the land?"

"I don't *care* about the land."

He cursed under his breath and scrubbed his brow.

Of course he cared, but...

Decided, he met her gaze. "I can't think about that now."

"It's that woman, isn't it?" Her slim nostrils flared. "How long have you known her?"

He told her the truth. "I met Maddy the same day I learned about Dahlia."

"Then she's a quick worker, getting you to agree to have her stay here."

"It wasn't like that."

Tara might have more reason than she knew to be jealous but it hadn't started out that way. Maddy hadn't set a trap to ensnare an eligible bachelor. She'd made a vow and had come to Leadeebrook when she would rather not have. Her loyalty to his sister, her indignation toward him, hadn't been an act.

Neither was the passion he'd felt break free when he'd held her last night. His palms had itched to shape over her curves. Conscience hadn't been an issue. The primal need to know every inch of her had overshadowed everything.

Tara was imploring him with her eyes.

"Tell me nothing's going on, Jack. Tell me and I'll believe you. You've made mistakes before." The passionate look wavered. "You don't want to make another one."

His eyes narrowed. He'd forget she said that.

"Tara, you and I are friends. I'll always think of you as a friend."

"Friendship can turn into love." She held his jaw and hitched up to slip her lips over his. "It did for me."

He found her hand and held it between both of his. "It's better this way."

He'd married once. He should have known that would do him a lifetime. The ring he wore around his neck would always live there.

But as he threw his hat back on and left the motel a few minutes later, he reminded himself that physical intimacy was another matter. No license was required to satisfy sexual needs. Needs every man had. Natural, instinctive. In this instance, fierce.

The chemistry was right between Maddy and him.

Yesterday under the stars, it had been near uncontainable. Whether this fever was due to the upheaval of emotion these past days—the lasting bond he and Maddy had shared with Dahlia—he couldn't say. All he knew with absolute certainty was he'd been attracted to Madison Tyler from the start. The attraction had grown to a point where, no matter what excuse he made, he couldn't deny it.

He wanted her in his bed.

The primal urge was a force unto itself, demanding release, stoking his mind like a stick at a fire every other minute of the day. He'd never felt this intensely about a woman, not even Sue. He'd never gone there with Tara, neither in mind nor in body.

After the way Maddy had held onto him in the moonlight, her fingers twisting in his shirt, her mouth opening under his, inviting and welcoming him in…

Inhaling, he slipped into his vehicle, ignited the engine and pulled away from the curb.

It was foregone. Maddy felt the same way. She wanted what he wanted. Before the week was through, he would convince her they should take it.

Call back. Urgent re Pompadour account.

Biting her lip, Maddy shifted her gaze from the text message to baby Beau lying, happy and energetic, on a nearby blanket.

Beau had had his lunchtime bottle but had been too restless to go down. She'd done some research; babies' routines changed all the time—teething problems, going to solids, natural decline in naps—all shook up what might seem like a set schedule. Rather than fight the tide, she'd spread a blanket out beneath the sprawling umbrella of a Poinciana tree and for the past twenty minutes had watched him kick and coo to his heart's content.

Although everyone back home knew she was unavailable, out of habit she'd brought along her BlackBerry. While her father had been frosty about her request for this unscheduled break, he wouldn't have left that message without good reason.

Maddy set the phone against her chin as her stomach flipped over.

Urgent…

Had Pompadour Shoes pulled the plug without having seen the campaign? Had another agency stolen their business? Or worse…had her father's disappointment turned to action? Had he replaced her on the account?

Her thumb was poised over Redial when Nell appeared out of nowhere and sat herself down a few feet away. Maddy's blood pressure climbed and she reached for Beau who, unconcerned, gnawed on a length of his rattle. But Nell's attention was elsewhere…fixed on the hazy distance, her ears perked high.

Maddy breathed—slowly in, calmly out.

If the dog wanted to sit around, okay. She didn't have dibs on this square of lawn, as long as Nell didn't get any ideas about wanting to socialize. But when Beau began to grumble, Nell trotted over and the hairs on the back of Maddy's neck stood up straight. Thankfully the collie didn't stop and soon Maddy knew why. The sound of an engine. The same sound she'd heard leaving the property early that morning.

Jack was home.

Maddy's heart began to thud. How would he tackle the subject of last night? Maybe he wouldn't bring up that kiss at all, which was fine by her. During the hours before dawn, she'd reflected enough on the blissful way his mouth had worked over hers. Useless thoughts had wound a never-ending loop in her mind, like what if Cait had discovered them? Where would it have led if she hadn't pulled away?

Maddy shuddered. The fallout didn't bear considering. If not another word was mentioned about that accident, she'd be happy. Surely Jack—a man considering marriage—felt the same way. As far as she was concerned, that caress never happened.

Nell belted a path out into the open space and a few moments later reappeared, ushering in the late model four-wheel drive. The vehicle braked and when the door opened, Maddy's limbs turned to jelly. Setting his Akubra in place, Jack angled out, looking taller and more formidable than she remembered.

Everything about him spoke of confidence and ability. Raw outback masculinity and pride. Good thing he *was* practically engaged or she might forget her resolve about last night's embarrassment and launch herself at him.

He made a motion. Nell rolled over and he rubbed her belly with the toe of his big boot. Patting her damp palms on her khaki pants, Maddy pasted on a nondescript smile. When Jack's gaze tracked her down, she gave a business-as-usual salute. He acknowledged her with a short nod and headed over. With each long, measured stride, her heart beat more wildly. She looked at those strong, large hands and felt them kneading her nape, pressing meaningfully on her back. She saw the shadow on his jaw and relived the delicious graze against her cheek, around her lips.

The next thirteen days would be tantamount to torture—not wanting to say goodbye to Beau, yet having to get back to Sydney. Needing to leave the memory of that kiss behind yet craving to know the sensation again. Talk about chronic inner turmoil.

Jack hunkered down beside the baby, his boots dusty and blue jeans stretched at the knee. When Beau's rattle slipped from his tiny grasp, Jack picked it up and shook the plastic keys until Beau grabbed and stuck one back in his mouth.

A side of Jack's mouth hiked up. "Guess he's hungry."

"He's had lunch. I think he's ready to be put down."

Jack tickled Beau's tummy and, enjoying it, the baby squawked and threw the keys down. Jack chuckled softly. "He looks like Dahlia. Same cheeky grin."

Maddy smiled. *Cheeky grins must run in the family.* Whenever Jack smiled at her that certain way, whenever his gaze dipped to stroke her lips, she could dissolve into a puddle, no problem at all. Guess he'd worked that out last night.

Cait called from the top of the stairs. "Want some lunch, Jock?"

Still on haunches, he swiveled around on the toes of his boots. "I'll get something later."

Cait nodded. "Can I put the bairn down for you, Maddy?"

"I can do it," Maddy called back.

But Cait was already on her way. "You can indeed. But he hasn't been out of your sight since seven this morning."

Jack scooped the baby up and gave him a little bounce in the air before handing him up to Cait.

Beaming, Cait brought him close. "Now it's my turn for a wee cuddle."

Beau looked so at home in Cait's arms, Maddy had no reason to cut in…except, after Cait and Beau's departure, she and Jack would be left completely alone. The idea set her pulse hammering all the more.

As Cait and the baby vanished back into the house,

Maddy gathered her highly-strung nerves. She'd simply have to deal with this situation in an adult-like manner. She'd offer a sentence or two while keeping communication friendly but unquestionably aboveboard. Then, after a reasonably short amount of time, she could follow Cait inside. Distance, and safety from possible humiliation and regret, accomplished.

With a blithe air, she collected her BlackBerry off the blanket. "Interesting that Cait calls you Jock."

"Jock. Jack. Jum. All short for James."

Maddy's insides clutched. Jack was James?

She remembered his reaction—the flinch—that first day she'd told him the baby's name. He and Dahlia hadn't spoken in years and yet she'd named her baby in part after her big brother—Beau James. Maddy could only imagine the stab of guilt when he heard. The gut wrench of regret and humility.

Her voice was soft. "It must've meant a lot to know Dahlia remembered you that way."

He removed his hat and filed a hand through his thick hair. "It was our grandfather's name, too. A family name. But, yeah, it was...nice."

Staring at his hat, he ran a finger and thumb around the felt rim then pushed to his feet. Squinting against the sun sitting high in the cloudless sky, he glanced around.

"Great day. Not too hot." He cocked a brow at her. "How about a ride?"

Maddy couldn't help it. She laughed. He never gave up. Which could be a problem if he applied that philosophy to what had happened outside the stables last night. But he hadn't needed convincing; when she'd put up the wall, reminded him of a couple of facts, he'd promptly taken his leave.

At his core, Jack was an old fashioned type. He'd had

an emotional wreck of a week. Their talk beneath the full moon—the comfortable, dreamy atmosphere it created—had caught them both unprepared. Now, however, they were fully aware of the dangers close proximity could bring. He was involved with another woman. Maddy had no intention of kissing Jack Prescott again.

She had less intention of jumping on a horse.

With a finger swipe, she alleviated her phone's screen of fine dust. "Think I'll leave the rodeo tricks to the experts."

"You don't have to leap six-foot fences. We can start off at a walk. Or we could double."

Maddy guffawed. With her arms around his waist, her breasts rubbing against his back… After seeing reason so soundly last night, surely he knew that suggestion was akin to teasing a fuse with a lit match.

"I'll get you riding," he went on, setting that distinctive hat back on his head, "even if I have to seize the moment and throw you on bareback."

The oxygen in her lungs began to burn. Quizzing his hooded gaze, she knew she wasn't mistaken. He wasn't talking about horses anymore and he wanted her to know it.

"In the meantime—" he offered her his hand "—what say I take you on a tour of Leadeebrook's woolshed."

Her thoughts still on riding bareback, Maddy accepted his hand before she'd thought. The skin on sizzling skin contact ignited a pheromone soaked spark that crackled all the way up her arm. On top of that, he'd pulled too hard. Catapulted into the air, her feet landed far too close to his. Once she'd got her breath and her bearings, her gaze butted with his. The message in his eyes said nothing about awkwardness or caution.

In fact, he looked unnervingly assured.

* * *

After a short drive, during which Maddy glued her shoulder to the passenger side to keep some semblance of distance between them, they arrived at a massive wooden structure set in a vast clearing.

"It looks like a ghost town now," Jack said, opening her door. "But when shearing was on, this place was a whirlwind of noise and activity."

Maddy took in the adjacent slow spinning windmill, a wire fence glinting in the distance and felt the cogs of time wind back. As they strolled up a grated ramp, she imagined she heard the commotion of workers amid thousands of sheep getting the excitement of shearing season underway. Sydney kept changing—higher skyscrapers, more traffic, extra tourists—yet the scene she pictured here might have been the same for a hundred years.

When they stepped into the building, Maddy suddenly felt very small and, at the same time, strangely enlivened. She rotated an awe-struck three-sixty. "It's massive."

"Eighty-two meters long, built in 1860 with enough room to accommodate fifty-two blade shearers. Thirty years on, the shed was converted to thirty-six stands of machine shears, powered by steam. Ten manual blade stands were kept, though, to hand shear stud sheep."

"Rams, you mean?"

"Can't risk losing anything valuable if the machinery goes mad."

She downplayed a grin. *Typical man.*

Their footsteps echoed through lofty rafters, some laced with tangles of cobwebs which muffled the occasional beat of sparrows' wings. Through numerous gaps in the rough side paneling, daylight slanted in, drawing crooked streaks on the raised floor. Dry earth, weathered wood and, beneath that, a smell that reminded her of the livestock pavilion at Sydney's Royal Easter Show.

Maddy pointed out the railed enclosures that took up a stretch of the vast room. "Is that where the sheep line up to have their sweaters taken off?"

He slapped a rail. "Each catching pen holds enough sheep for a two-hour shearing stint. A roustabout'll haul a sheep out of the pen onto a board—" he moved toward a mechanism attached to a long cord—powered shears "—and the shearer handles things from there. Once the fleece is removed, the sheep's popped through a moneybox, where she slides down a shute into a counting pen."

"Moneybox?"

He crossed the floor and clapped a rectangular frame on the wall. "One of these trap doors."

"Must be a cheery job." She mentioned the name of a famous shearing tune, then snapped her fingers in time with part of the chorus and sang, "'Click, click, click.'"

When his green eyes showed his laughter, a hot knot pulled low at her core and Maddy had to school her features against revealing any hint of the sensation. A wicked smile. A lidded look. Being alone with Jack was never a good idea.

"A great Aussie song," he said, "but unfortunately, not accurate."

Reaching high, he drew a dented tin box off a grimy shelf. Maddy watched, her gaze lapping over the cords in his forearms as he opened the lid. Her heart skipped several beats as her eyes wandered higher to skim over his magnificent shoulders, his incredibly masculine chest. When that burning knot pulled again, she inhaled, forced her gaze away and realized that he'd removed something from the tin—a pair of manual shears, which looked like an extra large pair of very basic scissors.

"A shearer would keep these sharper than a cut throat," he told her. "The idea wasn't to *snip* or *click*—" he closed the blades twice quickly to demonstrate "—but to start at a point then glide the blades up through the wool." He slid the shears along through the air.

"Like a dressmaker's scissors on fabric."

"Precisely." He ambled over to a large rectangular table. "The fleece is lain out on one of these wool tables for skirting, when dags and burrs are removed, then it's on to classing."

He found a square of wool in the shears' tin and traced a fingertip up the side of the white fleece. "The finer the wave, or crimp, the better the class."

When he handed over the sample, their hands touched. She took the wool, and as she played with the amazing softness of the fleece, she was certain that a moment ago his fingers had indeed lingered over hers.

"After the wool is classed, it's dropped into its appropriate bin," he went on. "When there's enough of one class, it's pressed into bales. In the beginning, the clip was transported by bullock wagons. From here to the nearest town, Newcastle, was a seven month journey."

Maddy could see Jack Prescott living and flourishing in such a time. He'd have an equally resilient woman by his side. As she gently rubbed the wool, Maddy closed her eyes and saw herself standing beside a nineteenth-century Jack Prescott and his bullock wagons. She quivered at the thought of the figure he would cut in this wilderness. Confident, intense, determined to succeed. That Jack, too, would conquer his environment, including any woman he held close and made love to at night.

Opening her eyes, feelings a little giddy, Maddy brought herself back. She really ought to stay focused.

"What do you plan to do with this place now?" she asked.

He looked around, his jaw tight. "Let it be."

"But it seems such a waste."

"The Australian wool industry hit its peak last century in the early fifties when my grandfather and his father ran the station, but that's over for Leadeebrook." His brows pinched and eyes clouded. "Times change."

And you have to move along with them, she thought, gazing down as she stroked the fleece. *Even if your heart and heritage are left behind.*

His deep voice, stronger now, echoed through the enormous room. "There's a gala on this weekend."

Her gaze snapped up and, understanding, she smiled. "Oh, that's fine. You go. I'm good to look after Beau."

"You're coming with me."

He was rounding the table, moving toward her, and Maddy's face began to flame.

They were miles from anyone, isolated in a way she'd never been isolated before. No prying eyes or baby cries to interrupt. That didn't make the telltale heat pumping through her veins okay. Didn't make the suggestion simmering in his eyes right either.

What was this? She'd wanted to believe he was a gentleman. An enigma, certainly, but honorable. Yet, here he was, blatantly hitting on her.

She squared her shoulders. "I'm sure your fiancée wouldn't approve of your suggestion."

His advance stopped and his jaw jutted. "I spoke with Tara this morning. I was wrong to consider marrying her. I said we should stay friends."

Maddy's thoughts began to spin. Clearly he'd broken off plans with Tara not only because of their embrace last night but because he had every intention of following that kiss up with another.

Whether he was spoken for or not, it wasn't happening. She hardly knew this man. While she was physically attracted to him—shamefully so—she wasn't even sure she *liked* him. And if he thought she was the kind to cave to temptation and fall into bed with someone for the hell of it, he was sadly mistaken.

"Jack, if this has anything to do with what happened between us last night…I mean, if you're thinking that maybe—"

"I'm thinking that while you're here, you might as well experience everything there is to offer. This is Beau's new home and you're our guest."

Was she a guest or, more than ever, a challenge?

Even as the consequences of such a thought burrowed in to arouse her, she shook her head.

"I'm sorry but I won't be attending any gala. I'm not here on vacation. It's not fair to leave Cait with Beau."

"You're going to have to leave Beau soon enough."

His thoughtful look—that fundamental statement—knocked her off balance and her hand, holding the wool, flattened on the table to steady her tilting weight.

Soon enough she *would* be gone. Depending on what lay behind her father's ominous text message, perhaps sooner than expected. Her pragmatic side said she should be grateful that Cait was so good with the baby and happy that Jack seemed to be resolved to forge a relationship with Beau. Happy her life would be going back to normal… back to Sydney at this crucial stage in her career.

"You'll need to pack a bag," he said. "It's a half hour flight from here."

Maddy's thoughts skipped back to the present. But he'd

lost her. Half an hour's flight? He was still talking about that gala?

"Why would I need a bag?"

"Simple." He stepped out from the shadows and a jagged streak of light cut across his face. "You and I will be staying the night."

Six

She'd been wrong. Jack wasn't self-assured. He was plain-and-simple arrogant.

To think he expected her to not only attend this gala affair with him, but also stay the night, made Maddy more determined than ever to stand her ground. She wasn't going. Fantasizing about throwing self-control to the wind and submitting to Jack's smoldering advances was one thing. Agreeing to spend the night together was quite another.

If it'd been any other man, she'd have laughed in his face. Or slapped it. But Jack wasn't any other man. He was a man of action who didn't see a thing wrong with going after what he wanted.

And it seemed he wanted her.

Thankfully during the drive back to the house he didn't bring the subject up again, although she was certain he hadn't taken her objections seriously. He kept sending out the vibes…lidded looks and loaded phrases that left her half dizzy and, frankly, annoyed. Yes, she'd let him kiss her—deeply. *Thoroughly.* That did *not* mean she had any intention of acting impulsively and stealing away with him…even if part of her desperately wanted to.

After dinner, Jack took Beau out onto the veranda for some cool air while Maddy stayed behind to help Cait.

"I'm good here," Cait told her, frothing soapy water at the sink. "You go keep Jock company with the bairn."

Not on your life. She'd copped more than enough of Jack's company—and sex appeal—for one day. Maddy flicked a tea towel off its rack.

"I'm sure he'd like time alone with Beau." She rescued a dripping plate from the drainer and promptly changed the subject to something safer. "I've been meaning to say… the nursery's beautiful. So fresh and the colors are just gorgeous." Pastel blues and mauves with clouds stenciled on the ceiling and koalas painted on the walls.

Dishcloth moving, Cait nodded at the water. "I washed all the linen and curtains when Jock let me know."

"Has that room always been the nursery? I mean, was it Jack's and Dahlia's room when they were babies?"

Cait's hands stopped milling around in the suds. "Jock and Sue…his wife…they did it up."

Maddy digested the information and slanted her head. "I didn't think Jack wanted a family."

"Did he tell you that?"

"In not so many words." When Cait kept her focus on the sink, a dreadful goosebumpy feeling funneled through Maddy's middle. What wasn't the housekeeper telling her?

"Cait?" She set the tea towel aside. "What is it?"

After two full beats, Cait slumped and hung her head.

"Sue wasn't the only one who was taken from Jock that night three years ago."

Maddy absorbed the words. When her mind settled on a plausible explanation, her hip hit the counter and a rush of tingles flew over her scalp.

Oh God. She closed her eyes and swallowed. "There was a baby, wasn't there?"

"A baby boy who was wanted very much. And to have that happen just a year after his parents' passing and Dahlia running off… He'd given up on the idea of family. Having a baby here at Leadeebrook…well, it's hard for him."

Maddy pressed against the sick feeling welling in her stomach. She could barely absorb it. "I wish I'd known."

"He doesn't talk about that day, though I'm sure he thinks about it often. Poor love, he blames himself."

Jack exuded the confidence and ability of a man who could defeat any foe or would die trying. Having to face that he hadn't been able to save his wife, his child…

Maddy swayed. She couldn't imagine the weight on his conscience. Perhaps it was similar to the guilt she felt about pushing Dahlia out the door that day to have her nails and hair done. Would she ever forgive herself?

Maddy dragged herself back to the here and now. Knowing this much about Jack's loss, she felt compelled to know more. More about how Jack's past might affect his relationship with Beau. More about the steel cowboy who was very much a flesh and blood man underneath.

Before she could ask, Maddy's senses prickled and she felt a presence at their backs. Heartbeat hammering, she rotated to face him.

Jack's impressive frame filled the doorway. The baby lay asleep in one arm. His other hand was bunched by his side.

"Beau's asleep," he said.

Maddy secretly gripped the counter for support. He'd come up on them so quietly...how much had he heard? She was so taken aback, she could barely get her lips to work.

When she'd gathered herself, she came forward and with her arms out to take the baby, she managed a smile.

"I'll put him down."

With a single step, Jack retreated into the hall. "I can do it."

Maddy's arms lowered. When they'd met, she didn't believe he had the wherewithal to care for this child beyond a grudging sense of duty. She certainly hadn't envisaged him being hands-on, wanting to change and feed and put Beau to bed. Initially, when they'd arrived here, she'd placed his insistence to help in the 'male pride' slot—he'd once run a sheep stud empire, therefore looking after an infant should be a piece of cake.

But she'd seen a shift in his attitude, like when he'd spoken about the baby's cheeky smile this afternoon, and when he'd lifted Beau out of the playpen to take him outside into the cool night. There'd been true caring in his eyes, a look that had touched a tender, hope-filled place inside of her.

Was he beginning to see Beau as a replacement for the child he'd lost? If so, wasn't that a healing move for Jack as well as a good outcome for the baby? Her head said yes.

Yet something niggled.

Jack moved off down the hall to put Beau to bed and Maddy returned to the sink. Whether he went to his room later or out to the stables, she didn't know but she didn't see Jack again.

Afterward, she went to her room and sat on the edge of her downy bed. She'd experienced a gamut of emotions these past few days. Guilt and deepest sadness over Dahlia's death. Fierce protectiveness toward Beau. Anger then curiosity toward Jack, followed more recently by acute physical desire and ultimately, tonight, empathy.

Slipping off her shoes, she took in her surroundings.

She didn't fit here, but Beau would—or did. The walls of this homestead contained memories, connections, history that were a part of who he was and Dahlia had known it. But this cozy quiet room, with its lace curtains, white cast iron headboard, patchwork quilt and rustic timber floors, was so not *her.* Madison Tyler was tailored suits and classic jewelry, multiple meetings and hardnose decisions. At this point in her life, Madison Tyler *was* the Pompadour account.

Exhaling, she studied her BlackBerry on the bedside table. Good or bad, she couldn't put that phone call off any longer.

Her father picked up with his usual abbreviated greeting. "Tyler here."

Maddy held the phone tighter to her ear. "Hey, Dad."

He groaned a sigh of relief. "Thank God. I need you back here *yesterday.*"

Holding her brow, she fell back against the quilt. Worse than she'd thought.

"What's wrong?"

"Pompadour wants to look at the campaign at the end of next week."

Her eyes flew open while her heart sank. "That's two weeks earlier than scheduled."

"They're eager to see what we have. I'm eager to show them." His voice cooled. "What about you?"

She visualized her big desk in her corner office suite even as she gazed at the vintage molded ceiling and felt today's soft fleece beneath her fingers. Then she heard Jack's plea...*you and I are staying the night.*

Her stomach knotted.

Her father wanted her to leave straight away?

"Maddy, you there?"

Thinking quick, she sat up. Today was Tuesday.

"The Pompadour proposal is polished and printed," she told him. "There's only the Powerpoint to tidy up and a final briefing with the staff involved. If I get back mid-next week, say crack of dawn Wednesday, that'll be plenty of time to pull those last strings together."

Tension crackled down the line. "Honey, I've been patient. I understand what good friends you were with that girl. But you've done what you promised. You've delivered the boy to his new home. Now it's time to get back to looking after you. Looking after your own future."

Maddy drew her legs up and hugged her knees. He was right. Absolutely. Given the circumstances, it was only logical she get back to her life, pronto.

Still...

She gnawed her bottom lip. "Dad, can you give me until Monday?"

She imagined her father shutting his eyes and shaking his head.

"You have a choice to make," he said, not unkindly. "Either come back and finish the job or I'll have to give it to someone who can."

Her throat closed. "But I've put so much work into that campaign." Storyboards, multiple media schedules, months spent on research both in Australia and overseas.

"This isn't about being fair. I love you, but that's personal. This is about business. You're either with Tyler Advertising a hundred percent or you're not."

She let go of her knees and straightened. "I understand."

She really did. And yet leaving Beau here after only one day seemed…worse than heartless.

As if reading her thoughts, her father sighed the way he used to when she was young and had pleaded for another scoop of ice cream after dinner.

"If you really think you can pull it off…all right. I'll give you 'til Monday to get back."

She pushed to her feet, beaming. "Really?"

"Monday eight a.m.," he decreed. "Not a minute later."

She said goodbye and thought over how thirteen days at Leadeebrook had dwindled down to five. At least she didn't have to hop on a plane back to Sydney as soon as tomorrow. But now she needed to make the most of every minute she had with Beau.

She crept the short distance down the darkened hall and when she reached the nursery, the door was ajar. After tiptoeing in, she waited for her eyes to adjust to the shadows and moonlight streaming in through the partly opened window. The outline of the crib grew more distinct as the smell of baby powder and Beau filled her lungs. Feeling the cool timber then soft center rug beneath her feet, she inched closer until her fingers curled over the sturdy cot rail. She smiled. Beau was sound asleep.

She stood there for she didn't know how long, simply drinking in the angelic form, filing this memory away for later. In this wedge of time, Sydney and Tyler's Advertising were another world away. Another universe.

And she was more than okay with that.

A creak came from behind. Heart zipping to her throat, Maddy spun around. A hulking shadow in the corner took on shape as it straightened out of a chair and edged toward her. She smothered a breathless gasp.

An intruder?

But as the figure drifted closer, its build became unmistakable. Of course it was Jack. Saying not a thing the whole while she'd been there.

"Why didn't you let me know you were in the room?" she whispered, hoping the irritation showed in her voice. No one liked to be spied on.

"I didn't want to disturb you." He came closer. "But when you stayed…"

He stopped beside her and his simmering magnetism at once drew her in. It was as if she were a planet being sucked into the heat of the sun, or the day needing to surrender to the unconditional blanket of the night.

Bracing herself, Maddy locked her weakened knees.

She needed to get out of here, away from him, before she did something foolish like let him kiss her again. She had to keep *focused*. But she needed to say something important—something that couldn't wait—before she left this room.

"I spoke with my father tonight," she told him. "He needs me back in Sydney early."

The dark slashes of his brows swooped together. "How early?"

"Monday morning."

His frown lowered to Beau. "How do you feel about that?"

She batted a reply around in her head and decided on, "I don't have a choice."

"Doesn't give me much time to get you in a saddle."

When he grinned, she gave in to a smile, too. *You wish.*

"But it *does* give us time for the gala," he went on. "Do you have a dress?"

Her jaw dropped and an exasperated sound escaped her throat.

"I seriously cannot believe you." The baby stirred. Gathering herself, she pressed her lips together and hushed her voice. "I'm not going anywhere with you, particularly not now that I only have five days left with Beau."

Even if, admittedly, when she'd spoken on the phone with her father and had asked for more time, going to the gala with Jack had been something of a consideration.

"Five days, yes," Jack agreed. "But that doesn't mean you can't come back."

The words hit her, caressed her, and she could only blink. Just days ago he'd barely wanted to know her and now…

She half smiled. "You want me to come *back?*"

"Now don't be shy. I know you're secretly attached to the Mitchell grass and the dust."

She almost laughed. Never, *ever* would that happen. But…

"I would like to come back and see Beau," she added to be clear.

"That can be arranged. On one condition."

She narrowed her eyes at him. "Is this going to be an offer I can't refuse?"

"Hope so." He turned to her and held her with his eyes. "Come away with me, Maddy. One night. Just one. Don't make me beg."

They'd known each other such a short time. But she was convinced of his strength and confidence and, above all else, his pride. The idea of him begging…

She touched her forehead.

He made her feel vulnerable. Desirable. *Hot.* How a woman should feel with a man. He almost made her feel too intensely.

"What are you afraid of?" His head angled and a lock of hair fell over his furrowed brow. When he moved closer, his height, his overpowering presence, seemed to curl over and absorb her.

"Once I thought I had all the time in the world," he murmured into the dark. "But we both know life isn't always that way. If we had more time, I probably wouldn't have suggested this." A corner of his mouth hooked up. "Then again, maybe I would have."

Her heart squeezed so much that it ached.

She was physically drawn to a ruggedly handsome man who wasn't hiding the fact that he was seriously drawn to her. He'd told her in the plainest of terms—he wanted them to spend the night together. He was saying he wanted to make love.

What did *she* want?

Not the girl who'd grown up without a mother, or the cosmo-chick who lived for her decaf soy latte each morning at eight. What did Madison Tyler, the woman, want?

He seemed to read her mind. His big hand threaded around her waist and brought her close. "This might help you decide."

His lips met hers, a feathery, devastatingly gentle caress. The steam in his blood found a way into hers and, in that mist-filled instant, she burned white-hot from the inside out. She told herself to keep her wits…to try to find her feet. Useless. Her defenses fell away and any remaining doubt drifted off like weightless wisps from a dandelion ball.

His mouth reluctantly left hers but the hold on her waist remained firm. When her eyes fluttered open, she didn't have the strength to even pretend she was annoyed. She understood the arguments. She barely knew him. She wasn't a leap-in-think-later type. God, what would Dahlia have thought?

And yet suddenly none of that mattered.

For so long she'd wanted to feel as if she truly belonged, without pressure, without fear of disapproval. Right or wrong, for one night she wanted to belong to Jack Prescott.

Siphoning in a much-needed breath, she sorted her thoughts.

"I'll go with you," she said, "but I have a condition of my own. That you don't do that again while we're under this roof."

His grin was lazy. "Was the kiss that bad?"

Her brows knitted. This wasn't a joke.

"I won't deny that I want you to kiss me again, because I do." At this moment more than she could ever have dreamed possible. "But if we start stealing kisses in every darkened corner, where does that leave Beau? The days that I'm left here, he deserves my attention. All of it." Maddy thought of Dahlia's trust in her—that sacred promise—and her throat swelled and closed off. "The least we can do is give him that much."

Jack's gaze turned inward before falling to the baby. A moment later, his hand left her waist. A muscle ticked in his jaw as he nodded.

"Agreed."

"But I will go with you on Saturday," she continued, "if we leave after he's gone down for the night and we arrive back early. Can you live with that?"

Jack studied Beau for a long moment before his gaze found hers once more. His expression changed. A knuckle curved around and lifted her jaw and for a strangled heartbeat Maddy thought he might kiss her again.

But he only smiled a thoughtful smile and murmured, "I can live with that."

Seven

The next day, back from his early ride, Jack headed for the house, remembering Maddy's words from the previous night. They'd rattled around in his head all morning. Had made him smile and made him wonder.

I won't deny that I want to kiss you again, because I do.

Maddy had agreed to go to the gala. In effect they both knew she'd agreed to more than that. Knowing he would soon take to bed the woman he'd been physically attracted to from the start left him with an acute sense of anticipation that released a new and vital heat surging through his veins. But their connection was more than physical. Had to be. He'd been intimate with women over the past three years. The acts had left his body sated, but not his mind. Not his heart. Something about Maddy affected him...*differently.*

Striding up the steps, he chided himself.

Of course he didn't kid himself that making love to Maddy could compare with what he and Sue had shared. It wouldn't, and that was as it should be. Neither could he pretend that he wouldn't have the hardest time keeping his promise not to touch Maddy again until Saturday evening. She wanted no distractions from her time left here with Beau. Commendable. But when they arrived in Clancy for the gala, he'd have to make up for lost time.

Stopping at the kitchen, Jack expected to see Cait by the sink or the stove, but the room, gleaming in the early morning light, was empty. Further down the hall, Maddy's door was closed. In passing, his pace slowed. He wanted to invite himself in. To break his promise and be done with it.

Scratching his jaw, he growled and moved on.

This situation was getting ridiculous. He shouldn't be so preoccupied with speculations over how Maddy would feel beneath him, her thighs coiled around his hips, her warm lips on his neck, on his chest. Family—now that he had one again—was what mattered.

He approached the nursery, confirming again in his mind that he wouldn't fail this boy. Not like he'd failed Dahlia when he hadn't brought her back all those years ago. But, hell, had rescuing his sister ever been possible? He might have been bigger. He might have been right. Staying at Leadeebrook was far safer for a girl—for Dahlia—than trying to survive on the outside. The rape, her death, proved that. But when Dahlia had left Leadeebrook, she'd been over eighteen. The law said she'd been old enough to make her own decisions, even if they ended in tragedy.

He stopped outside the partly closed nursery door and took stock. Life was known for irony, and that tragedy had also produced a baby, the only surviving link, other than himself, to the Prescott bloodline. Beau was more than

Dahlia's legacy, he was the Prescott future. Beau would grow up, find a nice woman, settle here at Leadeebrook, have a family of his own.

Jack pushed open the door, a smile curving his lips. He felt a great deal of comfort knowing that.

Kicking his heels, Beau was wide awake in his crib. After changing his diaper, Jack decided it was high time he took the boy on a tour. He bundled Beau up and headed for what had been known at Leadeebrook as the portrait hall.

"This is your great-great-grandfather," Jack said, stopping before the first portrait, which looked particularly regal in its gold-leaf gilded frame. "He was a determined and clever man. He and great-great-grandmother Prescott were responsible for making this homestead into the stately residence it is today."

Sitting quietly, gathered in his uncle's arm, Beau stared at the stern-looking gentleman in the frame before Jack moved further down the hall.

"And this," he said, pulling up in front of the next portrait, "is your great-grandfather. He taught me how to shear." Jack studied the baby then smiled and tickled his chin. "I'll have to teach you."

On the opposite side of the wide hall resided portraits of the Prescott women. He stopped at his late wife's and clenched his free hand to divert the familiar ache of loss that rose in his chest. The finest artist on the eastern coast had been commissioned for this piece, and the man had captured the loving shine in Sue's soft brown eyes perfectly.

At the same time Jack's throat thickened, Beau wriggled and he bypassed the other distinguished portraits until he reached the part of the house he visited often but always alone. After turning the handle, he entered the library—what had become Sue's library when she'd been alive. An extendable stepladder resided at the far end of the massive room. Numerous shelves, laden with all kinds of reading matter, towered toward the lofty ceiling. Designer crimson-and-yellow-gold swags decorated the tall windows. The cream chairs and couches bore the subtle sheen of finest quality upholstery.

This room upheld the Prescott promise of old money and impeccable taste, yet Sue had managed to make the library look cozy, too, with fresh flowers from the garden and bundles of home décor magazines and crossword puzzles camped out on occasional tables. The flowers were long gone, but the magazines he'd told Cait to leave.

Jack studied the baby studying the room. Beau was a smart kid. Even at this age, Jack could see it in his eyes.

"Will you be a reader or more a hands-on type like your uncle?" he asked his nephew, crossing to the nearest bookshelf. "Maybe both. Your mother was good at everything." He grinned, remembered when they'd been children. "Not that I ever let her know that."

He strolled half the length of the room to the children's section and eyed the spines that Sue might've read to Beau when he was a little older, as well as to their own son, had he lived.

Wincing, Jack inhaled deeply to dispel the twist of pain high in his gut. Every waking minute of every day, he missed her, missed what they'd had. And then Maddy had appeared in his life. When she was around, he didn't feel quite so empty, and he wasn't certain how to process that. Should he feel relieved or guilty?

The polished French-provincial desk in the corner drew his attention. He carried Beau across the room and slid open a drawer on the right hand side. The book was there...Sue's memory book.

Jack laid it out on the leather blotter and flipped through

the pages, pointing out Sue's relatives to a fist-sucking Beau. She had spent hours making the pages pretty. On the last page, a blue-and-yellow heart hugged a black-and-white image…a scan of their unborn child.

His eyes growing hot, Jack gently pressed his palm next to the eighteen-week-old shape that was his son.

"Sue wanted to name him after her father," he told Beau, in a deep, thick voice. "But I told her, no disrespect to her dad, that Peter Prescott sounded dumb. I'd wanted to name him after *my* father—"

A bitter nut of emotion opened high in his throat. Dropping his gaze, Jack swallowed hard and reached again for the drawer. He drew out a platinum-plated rattle, not a family heirloom but a gift Sue had bought for their baby a week before she'd died. The inscription read *Love forever, Mum and Dad.*

His chest tight, Jack smiled at the galloping horses etched down the cool handle. He shook the rattle and was rewarded by a sound similar to sleigh bells. At the noise, Beau pulled his ear then threw a hand out.

Lowering the rattle, Jack sank into the chair and, feeling empty again, searched his soul.

He examined first the scan image in Sue's book then Beau. Then he looked at each again. The pain behind his ribs intensified to a point where he almost lost his breath. But then, remarkably, the ache eased to a warm sensation rather than something bleak and cold and sour. He didn't want to feel that way anymore.

As the tension between his shoulders loosened, Jack bobbed Beau high on his arm and, pressing his lips to the baby's forehead, handed the rattle over.

Later that day, Jack was back in the stables, preparing to brush down Herc. But he was more interested in what was happening outside.

Beau was in the yard on a prickle-free patch of lawn and garden near the house. He was enthralled by the motion of the baby swing, which his uncle had hung from a tree branch that morning. Maddy pushed the swing, carefully—not too high. Her face was a portrait of joy. Of contentedness.

Smiling, Jack absently threaded Herc's brush strap over his hand.

Hell, no matter her mood, Maddy was attractive. Perfect symmetry, graceful movements. In his humble opinion, this landscape was the ideal foil for her skin and flaxen hair, particularly given the denim shorts and blousy blue top she wore today…the same color as her eyes. He itched to go join them in the dappled shade of that cypress. But simply looking from a distance raked the reawakened coals that smoldered deep in his gut.

True, they both felt the same fire. Both wanted the chance to turn the heat on to combustible high. But as much as it needled, he reminded himself yet again that she'd been right last night and he, in turn, meant to keep his word. He wouldn't crowd her. Foremost, she'd come to Leadeebrook to keep a promise not to begin an affair.

Jack turned to Herc and, frowning, swiped the bristles down his glossy black neck.

Affair wasn't the right word. Affair implied some sort of ongoing relationship and neither of them was immature enough to think that was a possibility. They lived thousands of miles apart. He didn't like the city. She was not a fan of the country. She might take up his offer and come back to visit once or twice. But she was a young woman with a life, and who she was and what she aspired to be wasn't here.

When Herc's flank twitched and his rear hoof pawed the ground, Jack swiped the brush again.

Good thing really. He'd considered taking on a more serious relationship with Tara and had concluded it would be a mistake. He'd had no choice but to take responsibility for Beau. After the initial king-hit shock, he was at peace with the arrangement. He'd do everything in his power to protect him, keep him close. Maddy, on the other hand…

Jack stopped brushing.

Well, Maddy was another matter.

Nell breezed by his leg, trotting out the door with a boomerang-shaped stick in her mouth. Curious, Jack crossed to the window in time to see Nell drop the stick at Maddy's feet.

It'd be a cold day in Hades before Maddy got chummy with a canine. Given her past, he couldn't blame her. He, however, couldn't imagine *not* having a dog around his feet. Not so long ago he'd owned five.

Her nose wrinkling, Maddy waved Nell back and Jack heard her say, "Shoo. Get away." But Nell kept sitting there, every few seconds nudging the stick closer to Maddy's city sneakers with her nose. Nell wanted to play. She could catch a stick for hours if anyone was silly enough to throw it. Nell thought Maddy was a good candidate.

Jack grinned.

And he'd thought Nell was smart.

He was about to rescue Maddy when she did the most remarkable thing. She stooped and, as if she were handling a stick of dynamite, lifted the no doubt slobbery stick between a single finger and thumb. With a move that reminded him a little of Swan Lake, she kicked out a leg at the same time she flung the stick away. With a visible shudder, she wiped her hand down her shorts' leg but before she could give Beau's swing another push, Nell was back, the stick between her jaws, eyes drilling her new playmate's.

When Maddy shrank back in alarm, Jack chuckled and set down the brush. Poor Maddy didn't know what she'd started. She was so much 'the lady.' Not prim, but rather manicured, French-scented, lipstick-in-the-morning female.

He liked that about her.

When Nell's ears pricked and she shot off into the western distance, Jack reached for his hat. Only one reason she'd leave her sport. Visitors.

By the time Jack had washed his hands and moved out into the true heat of the day, the familiar engine groan was unmistakable. Snow's Holden truck. Snow knew about Beau. The other evening, Jack had mentioned Maddy. Guess Snow'd gotten tired of waiting for an introduction.

Maddy had scooped Beau out of the molded swing seat by the time Jack joined her and Snow was alighting from his vehicle. Jack hadn't had time to explain to Maddy who their visitor was, although, from the white of Snow's beard, she might've guessed.

Snow didn't close the car door but rather clapped the thigh of his faded jeans. A lamb leaped out, landing in a spray of Mitchell grass with a scramble. Nell sniffed around the lamb but realizing the relationship between these two—this was not a sheep to be worked—she trotted back to her stick. But now Maddy seemed oblivious to Nell's insistent stare. Her own gaze wide, she clapped one hand over her mouth to catch an enchanted laugh. The lamb was prancing after Snow as if the crusty caretaker were his mother.

Snow offered his hand to Jack then announced in his tobacco-gruff voice, "Seeing you got a guest at your sheep station, Jum, I reckoned she might want to meet a sheep." Snow cordially touched his hat. "Snow Gibson at your service." He dropped a glance at his woolly companion. "This tagalong's Lolly."

Maddy introduced herself to Snow then, holding Beau on her hip, hunkered down. "Hello, there, Lolly." She combed her fingers between Lolly's fleecy ears and sighed. "You are the prettiest little darling ever."

Snow stroked his beard. "I see you got one of your own."

Maddy pushed up and spoke to Beau. "Say hello to Mr. Gibson, Beau."

Snow took the baby's tiny hand between a rough thumb and a stained knuckle. He sent Jack a hearty look. "He's like Dahlia."

His chest tight, Jack returned the smile. "Same grin."

"Think he'd like to see this other one fed?" Snow retrieved a bottle from his inside vest pocket. When he handed the bottle to Maddy, eyes sparkling, she sucked in a breath.

"Me?"

Wrinkles concertinaed down the side of Snow's face when he winked. "She'll be thirsty. You gotta hang on to this real tight."

Jack took Beau and both he and Maddy knelt down again. Lolly almost wrestled her over when she nuzzled up for the teat. As the lamb latched on, Maddy clung to the bottle with both hands while Jack considered a warm stirring emotion he had trouble naming.

He'd grown up with orphaned lambs as pets. Sue's parents had been farmers; livestock had been part of everyday life for both of them. He hadn't seen this kind of awed reaction over an animal in…he couldn't remember how long.

The emotion, he realized, was satisfaction.

With milk disappearing at a rapid rate, Maddy asked, "I didn't think there were any sheep left here?"

"I got a few," Snow expounded, "justa keep a hand in."

"You're a shearer?" she asked.

"Among other things, yes, ma'am."

"You'll have to give me a demonstration."

Snow shucked back his shoulders. "That would be my pleasure."

Beau squealed and thrust out an arm, fingers spread toward the lamb.

Snow chuckled. "The Prescott genes coming out."

Snow's Australian Services badge had lived on the side of his Akubra for decades. Now the metal glinted in the sun as he straightened his hat and put a question to Maddy.

"How you liking Leadeebrook?"

Jack's ears pricked. He'd like to hear her answer, too.

But, with a big smile, Maddy dodged the question with a throwaway comment. "Jack thinks he'll get me on a horse."

"Does he now?" Snow eyeballed Jack, who cleared his throat. Just because a man wanted to show a lady how to ride didn't mean anything, even if in this instance it did.

The lamb had finished his feed so Jack hooked a thumb at the house. "Might be time to get Beau out of this heat."

"Babies've got sensitive skin," Snow reflected, taking the drained bottle from Maddy. "But won't be too many summers before this one'll be flying off that tire swing hanging over Rapids Creek."

Maddy snapped a look at Jack. "There's a creek nearby?"

Snow confirmed, “Fulla water, too.”

Snow wasn’t being smart. There’d been times, and recently, when the creek bed had been bone-dry.

As they moved toward the stairs and the shade of the veranda, Maddy took the baby and slipped Jack an aside. “I won’t bother asking if the creek’s fenced.”

Jack wasn’t sure how to respond. Of course the creek wasn’t fenced.

“By law, pools have to be,” she told him. “Where children are concerned, I don’t see why creeks should be any different.”

Guess he wouldn’t tell her about the dams then.

He assured her, “My father taught me to swim before I could ride.”

“There are some excellent swimming schools and coaches in Sydney,” she countered in an encouraging tone.

He adjusted his hat and picked up his pace. “Beau doesn’t need to be an Olympian, Maddy. I can teach him everything he needs to know right here.”

“Everything?” She surveyed the endless plain with a lackluster air. “Here?”

He strode up the steps, half a length ahead. He wanted to tell his guest to let him worry about Beau. She was the go-between. He’d decide what needed to be done and he’d do it his way.

No mistakes this time.

Eight

Maddy hadn't known what to expect.

Hay stacks in every corner? Corncob bobbing contests? A country band wearing plaid shirts, plucking at banjos? Instead, that Saturday evening when she and Jack entered the Clancy City Gala Ball, she was more than pleasantly surprised.

Clancy was a Channel country community in Queensland's deep west. It boasted the usual small town landmarks. Nothing to write home about. But the exceptional establishment in which they now stood shone like an oasis in a desert. She might have been back in Sydney.

Amid the soft strains of tasteful pre-dinner music, uniformed wait staff breezed around classic timber decor surrounded by exquisite gold-plated fittings and waterfalls of fragrant floral arrangements. Best of all, their fellow guests alleviated any concerns she might have had about being overdressed.

Maddy's suitcase had presented nothing even remotely suitable to wear. Rather than rely on Hawksborough's sole boutique—Lindie's Labels—she had her assistant express courier a gown and accessories she'd purchased from a recent fashion show for an upcoming event. The alizarin-red chiffon sheath made her feel like a goddess.

The pleated shoulders were sheer with the waist gathered high under a cupped bodice, which created an elegant fall of fabric through the middle down to her silver-heeled toes. If her Bulgari crystal earrings added the perfect touch, Jack Prescott was the perfect escort.

As he took her arm to guide her through the mingling black-tie crowd, she enjoyed a thrilling rush of pride. The word hadn't been invented to describe the hold-onto-your-thumping-heart factor Jack oozed in that tailored dinner suit. Beneath the custom-made jacket, powerful broad shoulders rolled with every smooth measured step. His bearing was confident yet also casually relaxed. Movie producers cried out for masculine looks as dramatically chiseled as his.

Others in the room noticed, too. Women camouflaged their interest behind elevated flutes. Men stepped aside to give this naturally masterful guest right-of-way. Maddy had never felt more envied, more singled out or...*more special* in her life.

And this event was only the beginning of their evening. At the regional airport Jack had organized for their bags to be transported to an apartment he'd let for the night—a night she both anticipated with relish as well as with dread. A prude she was not, however, in her book, sexual intimacy wasn't something to be taken lightly. There was so much to consider. Her philosophy had always been that if it was going to happen, there was no need to rush.

Yet every time Jack looked at her she felt his gaze on her skin like a steamy caress. Every time he smiled, she wanted to surrender her lips up for his to take. Since Tuesday night when they'd made their pact to keep a respectable distance, the pressure to succumb had built until her anticipation surrounding tonight had tipped the scales toward flash point.

With his guiding arm through hers, she clasped her hands over her beaded pocketbook. As much as she'd lain awake in her patchwork quilt bed these past nights, staring at the ceiling and imagining what making love with Jack would be like, the imminent reality—the trip wire tight expectation of how this evening would end—now threatened to overwhelm her.

She'd bet her life he was a natural in the bedroom. Maddy was sure that as far as Jack was concerned, making love was an art form, a living masterpiece to be crafted with liberal amounts of sultry skill. She, on the other hand, wasn't entirely free of certain inhibitions. She wasn't the type to swing from chandeliers or even leave the lights on.

Would she disappoint him?

Through a break in the chattering crowd, a waiter appeared carrying a silver tray. Jack selected two flutes and offered one over. Maddy sipped the bubbles and sighed at the crisp heavenly taste.

He smiled. "You like champagne."

"A weakness, I'm afraid."

"Let's see...so that's chocolate custard, rainy mornings and French champagne."

She laughed. Tonight the deep timbre of his voice alone

was enough to leave her wonderfully weak. "I like books, too, don't forget."

His gaze skimmed her mouth. "I haven't forgotten anything."

"Jack, good to see you."

Maddy was snapped from her thrall when a man with a steel gray shock of hair thrust his hand out toward Jack.

Jack shook heartily. "Charlie Pelzer. How are you, mate?" His hot palm settled on Maddy's back. "You haven't met my date."

Maddy's smile wobbled. She wasn't sure if she liked being referred to as Jack's date. Or perhaps she liked it a little too much.

"Madison Tyler," she said cordially.

"Maddy's visiting from Sydney," Jack said. "She's in advertising."

Charlie's bushy brows fell together. "Your father's not Drew Tyler? He's a huge sponsor of one of my benefactors." He named a charity.

Maddy nodded, smiling. "I've heard him speak of it."

Charlie leaned in conspiratorially. "Perhaps you can bend his ear about sponsoring this cause."

He went into a spiel about The Royal Flying Doctor Service, how it was the largest and best aeromedical organization in the world and that without its dedicated staff and services, much of the outback would be uninhabitable. She hadn't realized that while the RFDS was government subsidized to a point, donations were needed to help replace aircraft and purchase supplies and equipment.

Knowing that they were here to support such a great cause alleviated some of the guilt she felt at leaving Beau for a few hours.

Charlie Pelzer and Jack discussed the position Japan

currently played in the Australian wool export market while Maddy happily sipped her champagne and enjoyed the lively atmosphere. She didn't dislike the quiet of the outback, per se. There was something undeniably peaceful about it. But this buzz felt like home.

When Charlie spotted another friend, he bowed off and Jack ushered her over to a long stretch of white clothed tables, upon which rested numerous prizes to be auctioned. Maddy's heartbeat fluttered as she inspected the nearby bidding sheets.

"I love silent auctions."

Jack gave an obliging shrug. "Then we'll have to do some real damage."

Holidays, boats, paintings, gym equipment. Maddy pulled up at a bizarre display. "Five cartons of beer?" Small glass bottles of the premium Aussie XXXX label.

Jack had signed many sheets. Now he swept a flourishing signature on this sheet, too, along with a ridiculous amount. Had the champagne gone to his head?

But his look said not to worry. "It's a tradition. A bit of fun."

The master of ceremonies called for guests to be seated. Maddy soaked up the conversation with their dinner companions, which included a criminal lawyer and a geologist recently returned from areas surrounding Uluru, or Ayers Rock as it was still known to many.

Guests continued bidding until the lot was officially closed and the highest bidder announced. The room erupted with applause when Jack was awarded the five cartons of beer. He also scored a painting by a well-respected indigenous artist. After a dessert of strawberry and passion fruit-topped Pavlova, the lights dimmed more and the music lilted into a familiar dreamy tune.

Jack pushed out his chair and offered his hand. "You like dancing, I presume."

Arching a bow, she accepted his hand. "I can hold my own."

But when he gathered her close on the dance floor beneath the slow spinning lights, it was clear who the expert was. Once his strong warm hand was wrapped around hers, he rested them both against his lapel while his other hand lightly pressed on the sensitive small of her back. As he began to lead, Maddy breathed in his delicious woodsy scent and, trying not to sigh, happily followed. She was so relaxed after the champagne and conversation at the table that she instinctively went to rest her cheek against the shoulder of his jacket.

His breath stirring her upswept hair, the magic of his body as he held her close and moved…it all felt strangely surreal. As if every one of her feel-good hormones had been released and her brain had no room for anything other than wondering how she could possibly get closer to Jack's unique brand of hard heat.

In time she pulled herself back.

Dangerous. They were in a room full of people who were clearly interested in the relationship between widower Jack Prescott and this new woman. To give them more to talk about wouldn't do, particularly given at least one of them knew her father. She didn't want it getting back that she was romantically involved or Drew Tyler could assume that romance was her reason for requesting those few extra days away.

Still…

Jack's chest felt so safe and his hand around hers felt so right. If she didn't want to stir any pots, her own included, it might be time to change the tone. A subject came to mind that had lain between them these past days. Now seemed the right moment to clear the air—as well as make her point clear.

"I hope you didn't think I overreacted the other day when I heard about the creek."

His step faltered almost imperceptibly before he continued to slow dance her around in a tight circle among other couples on the floor.

"I assure you," he said. "There's nothing to worry about."

Maddy chewed her lip. His wife and child both had died. She didn't know the specifics because Cait was reluctant to discuss it further. The last thing she wanted was to sound thoughtless, but the bottom line was that Beau's well-being had to be her main concern.

"I was only trying to point out that drowning can happen in a creek as easily as a suburban pool. Obviously nothing could be done to border off a creek," she rationalized. "As long as a good eye's kept on him at all times, I'm sure you're right. There'll be nothing to worry about." She couldn't help but add, "It's just that kids are known to wander off."

Which brought to mind a movie she'd seen long ago where a little boy had been lost in a desert. His lips cracked, blinded from scorpion venom, he'd wandered around, close to death, for days.

Feeling as if ants were crawling over her skin, she shuddered, then quizzed Jack.

"Does Australia have scorpions?" She had the biggest feeling it did. "I know we have snakes." Some of the deadliest in the world.

"Yes, we have snakes," he confirmed. "Scorpions, too, but in the bush we're down on murders and police car chases and high on helping each other out."

She took in his wry expression and let out that breath.

Yes, she should keep things in perspective. Growing up in the country wasn't necessarily a bad thing, or more hazardous than being raised in a city. She needed to keep telling herself that Beau would be happy in his new home after she had left and slipped back into her own life. This is what Dahlia had wanted for him…even if she hadn't wanted it for herself.

"You look beautiful in that gown," Jack murmured against the shell of her ear, clearly wanting to move on from that subject, too. "Everyone in the room thinks so."

Her heart swelled so much she didn't know if her ribs could contain it. Usually she was gracious in accepting compliments, but everything about Jack affected her more deeply. As her cheeks heated, she offered silent thanks for the muted lighting. She felt like a sixteen-year-old at her first dance with the boy every girl wanted to date.

Trying to make light of it, she shrugged.

"The color's quite striking."

"That's what I thought about your eyes when we first met."

A simmering kernel of want began to pulse in her core and she fell deeper into his mesmerizing eyes. He was so sexy, so handsome. Fatally hypnotic. With every passing minute, Sydney seemed farther and farther away.

With his thumb circling low on her back, he nodded at a point above her head. "Notice all the fairy lights."

She nodded. They gave the room an incredibly romantic feel, although that was more likely due to her dance partner's smoldering attention.

"Over there—" he tipped his head "—they've made a replica of the Southern Cross."

Arcing around, she took in the five larger lights which were patterned to reflect the star formation that was synonymous with Australian skies. She noticed some hazy, larger lights that seemed to hover upon the horizon of the room. "What formation are those meant to be?"

"You've heard of Min Min lights?"

She grinned. "Sure." The strange appearance of those lights in the outback was legendary.

He cocked a brow. "But did you know that Min Min light sightings are more prevalent in this district than any other?"

Her blood pressure spiked. In the fast-track world where she lived, Maddy didn't admit it often but she believed that not everything could be explained by science.

"Min Min lights were part of Aboriginal folklore long before modern day sightings made them famous," Jack said. "Experts agree the mysterious lights that show themselves to travelers at night aren't imagination. They appear in the distance, sometimes hazy, sometimes brilliant enough to light up objects around them. When you think you're getting closer, they can disappear only to reappear at your back, speeding up behind you, or at the side, seeming to watch."

Maddy involuntarily swallowed then tried to shake her dark fascination off.

"You're trying to scare me."

He chuckled and squeezed her hand. "Don't worry about them. I'm here."

Her blood flowed like hot syrup through her veins. But she straightened her shoulders and cast a casual glance around. Had anyone heard their conversation? Could anyone see her blush?

He tilted her face back toward him. "And I plan to keep you as close as possible all night."

Her breasts tingled and swelled, and she couldn't quite catch her breath. He was openly seducing her—*here,* amid hundreds of people. And the longer she drank him in, the more light-headed she became.

Giddy from the dance, from the music and from his charm, she dragged her gaze away.

"I...I don't know..."

His polished shoes stopped moving. With a firm hold of her hand, he headed for a set of glass doors and didn't stop until they stood on an otherwise vacant balcony surrounded by a dark velvet dome which held all the stars in the sky.

He faced her and his big palms sculpted over her shoulders, winging them slightly in as he held her still with a penetrating gaze.

"The last thing I want," he said in an earnest tone, "is for you to go through with something you're not entirely comfortable with." His intense hooded gaze lowered to her mouth. "So if you're uncomfortable—" he purposefully, slowly angled his head and his lips grazed hers "—even a little—" his lips brushed again and the hold on her shoulders tightened "—I can always stop."

Maddy's nerve endings shorted out. She couldn't get enough air. Her heart was smashing so madly against her ribs that surely he must have heard the wild thumping.

She'd made the decision to come tonight. She couldn't go back and yet she didn't know if she had the strength—the courage—to go forward. She felt small, unremarkable, like she had the day she walked into that woolshed. Jack was a thousand times more than any man she'd known. And despite the confident act, she was just Maddy.

And Maddy was less than perfect.

But when he drew her close and his mouth slanted possessively over hers, the trillion stars in the sky joined with the stars in her head. Sensations, glorious and absolute, spiraled through her, around her, and she dissolved then surrendered.

Her acceptance and commitment was complete. There would be no turning back. Now the only question seemed to be…

Would she ever want to stop?

He and Maddy arrived at their suite twenty minutes later.

During the cab ride, he'd held her hand in the back seat while she'd chatted on about how much she'd enjoyed the evening. Despite succumbing to him on the balcony—assuring him with the honesty of her caress of how she felt—she was nervous, and he wondered…

She was a city girl, mid-twenties, and worldly with it. He'd assumed she was practiced where men were concerned. Was it possible she was a virgin?

He *did* know that she looked incredible in that gown, particularly with her pale silky hair loosely swept up off her neck. Sensuous flowing fabric and glittering gems were her territory. She shone so brightly, she might have stepped off a New York runway. He'd had trouble keeping up with the conversation at the table, he'd been so bewitched by her grace and her beauty, and he didn't give a damn who'd known it.

Tara Anderson had appreciated glamour to a degree but she'd preferred breeches. He could identify. He was no stranger to tuxedoes but nothing topped the comfort of a pair of jeans and worn-in boots. Escorting Maddy tonight in that spectacular designer dress, however, had him revisiting that long held truth. He'd happily don a stiff collar if it meant having Maddy on his arm.

But, he had to remember, this wasn't an ongoing thing.

Inside the suite, she moved to the center of the expansive living room and rotated to face him. With her hands clasped high at her waist, the hem of her gown floated out and settled again around her slim ankles.

"Do you usually stay here for the gala weekend?"

"Always."

Although not in this room. He hadn't been to Clancy in three years. Hadn't been anywhere much at all. When he wasn't at Leadeebrook, he felt irritable. Out of sorts. Home was the only place that seemed to give him any reprieve from the constant rumble of regret that tagged him.

Rubbing his jaw, Jack crossed to the wet bar.

Did no good to let his mind wander in that direction. He'd loved his wife and where she was now, he was certain that she knew it. Long and hard he'd thought over his feelings for Madison Tyler. Hell, he'd over-analyzed them into the ground.

But he was happy with his decision. He wanted her here with him tonight. He only regretted that their time alone would be so brief. No use thinking about her next visit though—if there was one. Women of Maddy's caliber didn't stay free for long.

From the overhead rack he retrieved wine glasses.

Maddy's gesture caught his attention.

"You go ahead," she said. "But I'm fine."

He slid the glasses aside. He didn't want any more to drink. What he wanted was Maddy raveled up in his arms. He wanted to enjoy that heady, high altitude buzz she consistently whipped up inside him.

He wanted to feel her body, naked, beneath his.

Every minute they spent on small talk was one more precious minute wasted.

Intent, he moved toward her, tugging his bow tie free. When Maddy's eyes widened and her bodice rose on a silent breath, his step hesitated. What the devil was she afraid of? That he'd throw her down and take what he wanted? He didn't operate that way. If she'd only relax he'd be more than willing to show her.

He was an arm's length away when she spun on her heel to face the view of the town lights visible beyond the wall-to-wall window.

"I wonder if we'll see any Min Min lights tonight," she said. "You said they bob up around these parts all the time."

Jack rubbed the back of his neck. More than instinct said she wanted to be here. The way she'd danced with him, clung to him, wasn't manufactured. Yet something kept touching on her brakes. He'd assured her every way he could. With words, with affection.

Flicking back his jacket, Jack set his hands low on his hips. There were two ways to handle this...slow and ultra steady, or cut to the chase and let this push and pull game be decided upon once and for all.

He wound around to block her view before he folded his hands over hers. Bringing her cool knuckles to his lips, he warmed them with a heartfelt vow.

"Whatever you're worried about, believe me, Maddy, you don't need to be."

He meant that promise to the depths of his soul. He wouldn't hurt her for the world. He never wanted to cause harm to anyone again, consciously or otherwise.

She rolled her teeth over her bottom lip and Jack frowned. After coming this far he wondered if she might tell him now that she'd been wrong. That she didn't want to be with him as much as he wanted to be with her.

When she sucked in a breath and finally nodded, relieved, Jack smiled and nodded, too. At the same time, his glance dropped to her lips. Lips he'd remember forever.

His gut kicked with a familiar pleasant tug. This was right. *She* was right. Beyond ready, he lowered his head and claimed her.

Heat rose up his thighs, igniting a trail of flash fires over his skin. The urge to probe deeper, savor more, was alarmingly powerful, near impossible to resist. They were alone. His blood was booming. In his mind she was already writhing beneath him.

Kissing her still, his hands ironed up the curves of her waist. When he reached the bodice of her gown, his fingers encased her sides while each thumb stroked the underside of her breasts. As the kiss grew in intensity, his thumbs circled higher. While she whimpered in her throat and leaned in, he clenched every muscle to stop from satisfying the primal urge to pry those red cups apart.

Instead his mouth reluctantly left hers.

Her eyes were closed, her breathing labored. Her fingers dug into his biceps for support. The delectable burn smoldering below his belt expanded. These past days—watching her, wanting her—had been a bittersweet torture.

Angling, he scooped her off those dainty silver heels and up into the cradle of his jacketed arms. Her lashes fluttered open and his chest grew as she peered up at him with large, dewy eyes. Beyond a set of opened interior double doors, the master bed was in full view. The covers were turned down as he'd instructed. He'd find protection in the bedside drawer. With every cord in his body wound tight, he delivered her into the bedroom.

The room was dark, its open glass slider doors inviting in a cool breeze. Standing in shadows, he was vaguely aware of the moon's silver claw hanging in the sky, the night song of cicadas and a faint rustling of leaves. He set her on her feet, released his dinner shirt's top buttons and then stepped forward to find the zipper at her back. His hot gaze fused with hers, he eased the zipper down.

He felt her slight tremble as he edged one gossamer light sleeve off a slender shoulder then encouraged the next. The gown fell over her curves and landed in an airy puddle at her feet. Hungry, but patient, he soaked up the ethereal vision of her porcelain frame...her high full breasts, scanty red panties, long milky legs ending with sexy spiked heels. He inhaled to the bottom of his lungs then his gaze went to her hair.

"Let it down."

She hesitated only a heartbeat before reaching with both hands to release the pins. Her hair cascaded but she didn't shake out the kinks. Rather she looked to him as if waiting for his next move...or approval.

Stepping into the space separating them, he skimmed both sets of fingers up the column of her warm slender neck, carrying the hair high enough to leave ample access. Then he lowered his mouth to her throat and flicked her fast-beating pulse with the tip of his tongue.

She sighed and melted enough that he had to grip her upper arms to save her from slipping. With patience disintegrating, he carefully backed her up.

As she lowered to sit on the side of the bed, he studied her unwittingly erotic form. With his gaze slipping down the hair shimmering over one shoulder, he shucked back his shoulders and began to undress. Jacket first, shirt, and the rest. Then he knelt at her feet and slipped off her shoes.

Listening to her heavy breathing, high on the scent of her perfume, he closed his eyes and trailed his lips—moist, famished, lingering kisses—up her satin smooth shins, and higher...over her thighs, across her bikini line, around one hip—

He felt a lump. And another, like a welt. Frowning, he pulled back and jumped at the light switch. Dear God, had something bitten her?

The soft glow faded up at the same time he asked, "Maddy, what's wro—?"

The question stuck in his throat.

The scars were white, many and raised. Straight, jagged. Some were dots, reminders of deep puncture wounds. As his heart fisted in his throat, he found her pained face—cheeks red, eyes downcast.

Sick to his stomach, he ground out, "From the attack?"

She dragged the sheet up to cover what she could. Her hair fell in a pale blanket over her brow as she shook her head then shook it again.

"I know. They're ugly. Please..." She blindly flipped a finger at the switch. "Turn off the light."

But he found her free hand and pressed her palm to his cheek. Now it was clear. Now he understood. This why she'd seemed so uncertain.

He brushed his lips over her inside wrist.

"Maddy, do you think that could make a difference to how I feel?"

She slowly looked at him, question marks in her searching gaze. He gave her time to absorb the honesty in his eyes then she let him ease the sheet down.

He kissed the marks. Each and every one. After a time, when her fisted hands relaxed and her stiffness eased, he continued up until his mouth found and captured hers. He maneuvered her back until she lay flat and as she wound her hands through his hair, he pressed in, kissing her as desperately as she was now kissing him.

His descending touch found her more ready than he could have hoped. She was swollen, so wet. He wanted to explore her, enjoy her, with everything she might crave and he so badly needed to give. He lowered her panties as his mouth trailed a seductive line down her neck to her breasts.

His fingertip drew tiny pressure circles round the bead above her folds while his tongue twirled over her nipples. Her nails alternately skimmed or dug half moons into his back. Every so often she made little noises that shot flaming arrows to his groin. Soon she was grinding her hips into the sheet or curling them up to intensify his touch.

The second she tensed and her hand came over to hold his in place, he drew back and saw to protection before he joined her again. Searching her eyes in the shadows, he opened her with his fingers then eased partly in.

She tightened around his tip. As she squeezed around him, her hands filed up the plane of his chest, her fingers fanning and winding over his muscles. Something tinkled. The wedding band on his gold chain. He stopped, visualized the ring and what it stood for but when she began to breathe again, that image faded and he continued to move…a little deeper, a little harder.

Every inch of him was steamy and his heart was a fast-pumping piston by the time he brought her leg high over the back of his thigh. Her calf clamped down to hold him firm. Reading the sign, he drove in all the way.

The fit was glorious, the impulse to give in was mind blowing. The mighty force to reward physical necessity was an avalanche crashing on his back. Clenching every muscle, he tucked in his chin until it met his chest, but it was no good. This was way beyond control.

When she stilled, too, she set off a chain reaction he couldn't prevent. She gave a breathy pant of air, a delicious, full body shudder. Then she threw back her head and her hips jutted off the mattress. Double-gripping the sheet, Maddy cried out and Jack's long-anticipated landslide pushed through.

The release was so complete it seemed to tear his every fiber apart at the same time a primal sound squeezed from his chest. Circling his arm above her head, he swallowed her sigh with a penetrating kiss. Lost in sensation, soaring on the high, Jack scooped his other arm beneath her back and dragged her closer still. Deeply physical, gloriously fierce. This was a passion the likes of which he'd never tasted before. And must taste again.

Nine

Later, still floating from the effects of their lovemaking, Maddy lay with the sheet draped over her legs, drawing lazy circles through the crisp dark hair that dusted Jack's chest. With his arm around her and fingertips trailing up and down her side, she thought over the amazing time they'd spent together in this bed. Her anxiety had been unwarranted. He'd discovered the scars but hadn't been revolted. In fact, she'd never felt more adored.

Her hand wandered higher, into the warm beating hollow of his throat, and her fingers met with the cool of the chain he wore and the circle of the ring threaded through it.

A gold ring.

Maddy stilled, then her palm flattened and slid down to rest on the hard ridges of his abdomen. She'd seen the wedding band before, when he'd taken off his shirt that first day in the nursery, but with so many other things crashing through her mind, she'd thought little of it.

Did he ever take the ring off? If he hadn't tonight, when making love with her had been his intention, she guessed not. Did he wear it around his neck to keep it close to his heart?

Although he didn't show his feelings often, Jack Prescott was a man capable of deep emotion. Of deep loyalty. Some people gave their heart to only one person in their lifetime. Jack had obviously found his soul mate. Had found her and then lost her three years ago.

Maddy's brow pinched and her stomach knotted.

Where did that leave *her* in his affections?

But she shook herself. Tonight wasn't about eternity. He'd never intimated that it was. After knowing each other a week, how could it be?

The ring around his neck was an acknowledgement as well as a sign that couldn't be mistaken. What they shared was a mountain above wonderful but their time together here was based on physical attraction. The electricity that crackled between them was real, was strong. But, where it counted, that ring said he would always belong to someone else.

She breathed in his woodsy masculine scent and snuggled closer.

Still, she couldn't regret agreeing to this arrangement. He wasn't wearing that ring to hurt her. The simple truth was that she wouldn't have missed these past hours for anything.

She'd read about men who made love the way Jack did. Unselfishly. Finding so much pleasure in giving. He'd lifted her to another sphere of awareness, of passion, where more than bodies had joined. She'd never felt closer to another human being. The feeling of absolute rapture would live with her long after tonight was over. So would his reaction after his lips had grazed her hip.

He'd been so supportive when he'd discovered her scars. The last man she'd come close to being intimate with had recoiled in horror. She'd dated that guy for five months. She thought she'd known him. Had wanted to trust him.

Did anyone ever truly know someone else?

Heck, when it came down to it, maybe Jack was just a really good actor.

Easing the sheet higher, she murmured against his chest. She had to ask.

"Those scars are pretty scary, huh?"

"The scars aren't scary." His chest hardened more as he craned to brush his lips over her crown. "What you must have gone through would've been."

A cold shaft whistled through her center and Maddy shut her eyes. She didn't like to think about that day. Whenever the memories surfaced she pushed them down as far as she could. But now she lifted the lid a little and dared to let them rise.

The images were fuzzy.

What had she been wearing? She'd been riding to the shop, but to buy what? Milk, perhaps. Bread. She thought harder but didn't shudder, not like she used to whenever memories had crept up and caught her unawares. The nightmares had been the worst.

"I fell off my bike," she said and realized she'd spoken aloud. "The dog was on me before I could find the handlebars. The real pain didn't hit until later. There was no internal damage."

He tugged her close and spoke against her hair. "Something to be grateful for, I suppose."

Other recollections swam up.

"The doctors and nurses were great. I was a long time in

the hospital. When he visited, my dad's face was lined with guilt. He'd given me the bike. Said with lots of practice I'd get better. I was a bit of a klutz."

"You wouldn't know it now. You move like a vision."

She laughed softly. "I do not."

"Believe me, you're not that klutzy kid anymore. You're a very desirable woman."

She laughed again. "*Very* desirable."

"Very, very desirable. That's something that comes from inside."

In the shadows, she pushed up on one elbow. When she found his eyes, she sent him a mock chagrined look. "You're such a charmer."

"Are you doubting my sincerity? Because if you are—" he shifted until his nose was an inch from hers "—I should show you how serious I am."

His kiss was tender and at the same time held more meaning and passion than any other. At that moment Jack wasn't Dahlia's brother, or Beau's uncle, or even an enigmatic, sexy-to-a-fault grazier. He was the man who'd transformed her into the most beautiful woman in the world. And the feeling was fairy tale fabulous. It was also almost sad.

No one would ever be better than Jack.

When her throat closed off and emotion pricked behind her eyes, Maddy broke from the kiss and wriggled out from beneath him.

Hormones. One minute she was floating, the next she wanted to cry. Too much excitement. Too much emotion. She needed to take a few deep breaths and focus on something else.

When her feet sunk into the soft carpet, she dragged the sheet along with her. "I wonder what Beau's doing now?"

"Sleeping. Where're you going?"

"To get some fresh air."

She moved out onto the balcony where the smattering of town lights twinkled below and mournful curlews cried out in the distance. She was still thinking about Beau when something soft and warm wrapped around her shoulders. Then big hands raveled the blanket around her middle and pressed in.

Jack's deep voice was at her ear. "It can get chilly out here at night."

"I hope Beau's warm enough. Maybe I should have put him in his fleecy PJs."

Chuckling, he grazed his chin over her hair. "You're quite the mother hen, aren't you?"

"He's a cute kid." She smiled into the night, remembering way back. "He reminds me of a life-size baby doll I used to have."

"Dolls, huh? Dahlia liked skipping. One summer she skipped so much I thought her brain would get shaken out of her head."

"And she liked horses?"

"Sure." There was a pregnant pause. "You should try it."

Grinning, she wrestled the blanket more firmly around her. "The day I get on a horse, Jack Prescott, is the day I change my name and dance the polka."

His smile grazed her temple. "My mother didn't like horses much either, even though she'd ridden since she was five."

"How did your parents meet?"

"At a dance. My mother was visiting a cousin. My father fell in love with her on sight." He grinned. "Or that's what he told us kids."

She imagined a couple thirty-odd years ago locked in each other's gazes and an intimate embrace while they moved around a dance floor. The man she imagined looked a lot like Jack. A heart-warming glow filtered through her and she smiled.

"I bet your father treated her like a queen."

"He'd have given her anything she wanted," he said, "But she didn't want a lot." He exhaled and his tone changed. "She had a dream of taking a long vacation on an island. She had a thing for that movie *Endless Love.* Dad booked the flight without her knowing. They'd only been gone a week when she went out swimming and got in trouble. He went out to help."

Maddy held her sinking stomach and pivoted to face him. So that's how he'd lost his parents.

"Jack…I'm so sorry."

Even sorrier that she'd spoken up so strongly about that creek. After losing his parents to a drowning accident she was sure he would rather die himself than risk placing Beau in similar danger. Or any danger, for that matter.

Her palm fanned over his hot bare shoulder. "It must have been hard losing them both."

His eyes glistened in the shadows. He didn't seem to be looking at her but rather through her. "Dahlia didn't take it well."

"Is that why she left for Sydney?"

That bronzed shoulder lifted and fell. "She said she didn't want to be stuck at Leadeebrook like Mum had been all her life. She wasn't going to be trapped." A humorless smile tugged one side of his mouth. "My sister didn't get that if Mum and Dad had stayed on the station they'd still be alive."

Maddy angled her head. Had she heard right?

"Jack, you can't look at it like that. Your parents were on vacation, a well-deserved one, I'm sure. It was an accident."

"An accident they could've avoided."

The line of his mouth hardened and he didn't say the rest although Maddy could guess. *Like Dahlia's accident could've been avoided if she'd stayed at home.*

She had to know for Beau's sake.

Taking his hand, she turned so he held her again while they gazed out over the peaceful outback view. A falling star trailed through the star-studded sky.

"I was speaking to Cait about the nursery," she began. "She told me that you and your wife decorated it."

When his silence stretched out, Maddy cursed herself. She shouldn't have brought it up. If he told her not to speak of it again she wouldn't blame him. Three years was a heartbeat when you were trying to get over a tragedy. She knew.

She'd accepted that he wouldn't reply when his deep voice rumbled over her head.

"The contractions started at three in the morning. She was so excited and anxious. I reminded her that we were a month from the due date. On our last visit the doctor explained about Braxton Hicks. Basically false alarm contractions. A storm was raging outside. The contractions eased but she wanted to go into town and check with the doctor. Her own mother had died in childbirth and now she couldn't seem to think of anything but that. I tried to calm her. Told her we'd wait until light. When she started to cry…" He groaned and exhaled slowly before ending. "I packed her up and headed off. A tree came down on the car. I lived. Lesson learned."

Maddy was holding her stomach, her moist eyes shut. She couldn't bear to think of his pain.

"What lesson is that?" she finally got out.

"Don't tempt fate."

"But no one could guess such a terrible thing would have happened."

"Terrible things seem to follow me around."

Maddy's heart fell. She'd never felt more pity for anyone in her life. He'd lost everyone he'd loved including his unborn child and he blamed himself because he couldn't control the uncontrollable. No wonder he wanted to lock himself away from the world, somewhere he believed he and his memories could be safe. He so desperately wanted to go back in time and make everyone else safe there, too.

But he'd ventured beyond Leadeebrook boundaries tonight. He'd wanted to share an experience with her, the gala, dancing…making love.

"None of those things were your fault," she said, wishing he could lower his defenses for a moment and see.

"Doesn't change the fact that the people I loved most are gone."

She turned in the circle of his arms and held his gaze with hers. "If I was in trouble, if I needed someone to be there to rescue me…I'd choose you."

His gaze softened only to darken more. "And if I failed?"

"Then no one could have saved me."

Maddy thought of her mother, how the leukemia had won; Helen Tyler had accepted her fate even when her husband had begged her to fight. By being strong now—for her father, for her future—in some weird way Maddy felt as if she was making her mother strong, too, and fixing what no one could fix back then.

She'd never admitted those feelings to anyone. Would Jack understand if she told him?

When she shivered, he scooped her close and whispered in a deep sexy drawl, "Come back to bed."

After they moved inside, they made love again, and this time was even better than the first. Then they talked. Talked until dawn. About school days and old friendships. About far-reaching hopes and some of their dreams. When she told him about her father and then her mother's illness—how she wanted to be strong for her now—he brushed the hair from her cheek and with the softest smile said he understood.

When she and Jack arrived at Leadeebrook at seven the next morning, Maddy was bleary-eyed from lack of sleep. She was also pulsing with new energy and heartsick about leaving the next day.

The time had gone too quickly. Even the dry heat and the dust were somehow welcome today. A part of her was even glad to see Nell darting out to greet them.

As they made their way up the front steps, the bold eastern sun warming their backs, Maddy was gripped by an overwhelming need to have this day stretch out like an endless piece of string. She couldn't think of another way to put off the flight she'd booked for herself for Sydney.

Jack had offered to fly her but she'd declined. Saying goodbye here would be tough enough. If he flew her home, she'd be tempted to ask him to stay. Or to ask if she could fly back with him.

Ridiculous.

She'd had one heck of a week at Leadeebrook Station and, to top it off, an unbelievable time last night. The hopeless romantic inside her wanted to be swept up into that spell again. But the responsible woman knew a rerun wasn't possible.

Or was it?

The notion of spending more time here with Jack ribboned around her like a bright new promise and Maddy's face flushed with hope and shame. The basis of Jack's offer for her to return to Leadeebrook had been to visit Beau. She'd been so happy and relieved when he'd suggested it. She'd dreaded the thought of not knowing when she'd see the baby next. After the incredible hours spent in Jack's arms last night, was it wrong to speculate on other advantages?

But if she *did* come back, and she and Jack had another fling, how would she define their relationship? They wouldn't be a couple. She wouldn't be a friend. Maybe a "friend with benefits."

The less contemporary term was mistress.

They reached the top of the steps at the same time that Cait brought Beau out.

The bright-eyed housekeeper held the baby, his back to her front, so that Beau could see all the action. His little legs in their Mickey Mouse cotton PJs pumped with excitement when he saw them. They might've been gone a week.

Cait laughed. "He must've heard the plane. He just woke this minute."

Maddy's arms, but more so her heart, reached out. She'd missed him—his chubby cheeks, his soft curly top. Now she realized how much.

"Did he sleep through?" she asked, taking him from Cait, reveling in his beautiful baby smell while he gazed up into her face and she smiled lovingly down.

"Not a whimper, the little pet." Cait stepped aside to let Jack by with the bags. "How was the gala?"

Before Jack could answer, Maddy piped up, "It was *wonderful.*"

Too late, she zipped her lip.

The sparkle in Cait's eyes confirmed what Maddy had feared. Her abundance of enthusiasm at having spent the night alone with Jack had come across loud and clear.

But she wasn't in love. People didn't fall in love after a week.

Did they?

Maddy wasn't sure if it was her imagination but when the hands of her watch reached four and she hadn't seen Jack since scones and morning tea, she was certain. He was either letting her have quality one-on-one time with Beau or he was avoiding her.

In the kitchen, absently sealing the top on Beau's bottle, she wondered. She didn't want to consider the possibility but...did he regret last night?

She rotated toward baby Beau and kissed his tiny fist as he sat patiently in his reclined baby chair.

Jack's feelings couldn't have changed. What she'd felt and what he'd given hadn't been a lie. There was a good explanation for his absence today. Maybe Snow had got in trouble in some distant paddock. Perhaps Jack had fallen off his horse. He could've broken a leg.

She set the bottle on the table, failing to swallow the prevailing sense of doom rising in her throat. Today was her last here. After the intimacies they'd enjoyed, the words they'd said, Jack *must* want to share these remaining hours with her.

As much as she wanted to share them with him.

Maddy lifted Beau. Once nestled against her, with a happy mew he latched onto the bottle and his perfect dimpled hand curled over it. Maddy cradled the baby, drinking in his innocence and, at the same time, holding her breath to stop the spiral of doubt from winding any higher.

She'd been in Beau's life from the moment he was born. She'd been there with Dahlia when he'd come into the world. She'd rocked him and burped him and played "little piggie" long before coming here.

She *loved* this little boy. She would give her life for him in an instant. And when someone loved a child, that love didn't disappear. This kind of love was forever; her heart of hearts told her that. She may not be Beau's mother but that didn't change the way she felt. He was the most precious person in the world to her.

And Jack?

Closing her eyes, Maddy sighed remembering his smile, his woodsy scent, the thrilling rush that flooded her body whenever she saw him. Whenever he held her. Had she fallen in love with this ruggedly handsome man when a week ago she wanted to throttle him? She hadn't understood a thing about him then. She hadn't wanted to.

But here she'd come to know a different side of Jack Prescott—a side that was dedicated to his nephew, had cared deeply for his sister, had been a loving husband and was a heartbroken widower.

In Clancy she'd learned more. They'd spent amazing hours, laughing, talking, making the most blissful kind of love. His kisses sizzled with soul-soaring passion and yet each caress was defined by the purest strain of tenderness. The sensation of his hard, long body locking with hers… the reality of just how effortlessly he brought out every hidden, wanting part of her…

She'd been lifted to the clouds.

Would any woman feel differently, or did she and Jack share something truly special?

She opened her eyes and searched out the kitchen window.

Why wasn't he back?

* * *

Beau was still down for an afternoon nap when Jack rode in near sundown. Through a sitting room window, Maddy tracked his rolling stride as he led Herc to the stables. The horse's nostrils flared from exertion, and his coat was glossy with sweat. Jack would be out there with him for some time yet.

A startling urge leapt up inside of her and she gripped the window sill.

How would Jack react if she appeared at the stable door and asked what had kept him? After these hours of waiting and worrying, she needed to see for herself if the affection that had shone in his eyes last night had dimmed. Could he block out, as easily as this, the way she'd murmured his name?

Fifteen minutes later, she was chewing a thumbnail, pacing the hall, waiting for Beau to wake. She was stir-crazy. An unraveling ball of frazzled nerves. Over a man she'd known a few days and who hadn't chosen to spend these last hours with her.

Clearly she needed to get back to her friends and throw herself back into work. Remember who she was and where she belonged, which wasn't here in this barren wilderness.

She stopped at the front door, hands bunched at her sides. She flicked a glance at the still-quiet nursery, heard Cait's saucepans' distant rattle in the kitchen. The sinking sun washed pails of luminous orange, red and mauve across the hushed horizon. The night was fast approaching. Soon the morning would be here.

Maddy's hands bunched tighter.

Would he *ever* come in?

Her frayed patience snapped. She marched down the stairs and cut a bee-line to the stables.

Jack sat at a small table, dusty boots balanced on one end, ankles crossed. He was rubbing down some leather strap or other, but now the action stopped. His head turned and his wary gaze met hers.

Quivering inside, she stepped forward. In his stall, Herc shook his mane. Her stomach jumping, she pulled up abruptly then scolded herself.

Don't let him know your knees feel like water. Don't let him see you're upset.

Manufacturing a smile, she tipped her head in the homestead's direction. "Dinner's almost done."

His boots swung off the table and the front legs of the chair smacked the wood. "Great. I'm starved."

With that smooth rolling stride, he moved into the tack room and emerged several minutes later. When he didn't acknowledge her but rather crossed to flick his hat off a peg, she cleared her throat quietly, just enough to be sure her voice wouldn't crack.

"There's rhubarb pie for dessert," she said. "Smells delicious."

He dusted off the brown felt then gifted her a tight smile. "Can't wait."

"In a couple of month's Beau'll be tasting solids. I wonder if he'll have a sweet tooth."

"You must leave me your address." He fitted his hat. "I'll let you know how it goes."

When he continued to stand several paces away, the chiseled planes of his face so impassive, her heart contracted and then slid to her feet.

She couldn't stand the tension a moment longer. They needed to talk, sort this out, whether he liked it or not.

"Jack, I'm confused. Have I done something wrong?"

His brows flew together. "Of course not."

"Then where have you been all day?"

He removed his hat, glared at its well while he shoveled a hand through his thick black hair. "I had things to do."

"What things?"

"You wouldn't understand."

"What wouldn't I understand?"

His hat dropped to his side as he heaved out a breath. "Do you really want to know? You're going back tomorrow." He threw a glance around the stable walls. "This'll all be a dusty memory in a month."

Maddy's breath double hitched in her chest.

What was going on? Why was he suddenly so cold? So hurtful? Because she was leaving? He'd always known that.

She moistened her dry lips and reminded him, "You invited me to come back."

"You can come back any time you like," he said blandly.

The room tilted. Had she *dreamt* last night? This Jack was like a different man.

"Can I get this straight? You're saying you're not bothered either way? Whether I come back or not?"

"It's up to you. You have your life. You know what you're doing with it." He glanced at his watch. "And we'd better have tea so you can pack and get back to it."

He headed for the stable door but his pace slowed when she didn't follow.

Her feet were lead blocks. Her insides were roped with heavy knots. She could barely stop the corners of her mouth from bowing. Where was the man she'd shared so much with last night?

Was she supposed to nod politely now and eat dinner at the table as if nothing had happened? As if he hadn't nuzzled and stroked every inch of her? As if he hadn't opened up each hidden part of her soul and invited himself into her heart?

Dammit, if he thought he could walk away from this that easily, he was wrong.

"I need you to answer me. Do you want me to come back?"

His eyes didn't meet hers as he growled over one broad shoulder, "Of course I'd like you to come back."

"Jack...*look at me.*"

His broad back in the sexy chambray shirt expanded as he inhaled. He slowly turned. Rubbed his jaw. Met her eyes.

A muscle popped in his darkly shadowed square-cut jaw. "I'm not sure what you want."

She didn't give herself time to think. She walked straight over to cup his face. Then, bouncing up on her toes, she kissed him.

For an instant she felt that same fire, the spark-to-gas-leak explosion that had ripped through and released her again and again last night. She imagined she heard a rumble of satisfaction deep in his chest, felt the vibration rise in his throat and tingle with crystal clear meaning across her lips.

But as suddenly as it appeared, the scalding tension slid away and the kiss...his mouth on hers...lost its life.

The fire was gone. Snuffed out. Or had he simply locked it away behind a steel door? After the heartfelt promise he'd made—that whatever she was worried about, she didn't need to be—could he hurt her that way now?

Gutted, she let go of his jaw, found her feet and stepped back. But before she looked into his eyes, she willed all emotion from her face. She thought of scorpions and snakes. Of barren dusty miles she would soon say goodbye and good riddance to forever. The alternative was to break down and cry and…

She eased out a breath.

She'd rather be strong.

He'd said he didn't know what she wanted.

Shaking back her hair, she pasted on an unaffected smile and formed the necessary lie in her head.

"Oh, Jack," she began, "be fair. All I want is for you to know how much last night meant. Every girl dreams of having a real cowboy." She raised a playful grin. "And you're as real as they get." When tears stung like acid behind her eyes, she smiled harder and rubbed her nose. "I'm going to have to get out of here before I have a sneezing fit."

She brushed past before the tears caught up and beat her down. Damned if she'd let him see her cry.

"Maddy, *wait.*"

Spinning around, she theatrically pinched her nose. "I sincerely hope you're not going to ask me to help clean out that stall or brush down Herc."

They shared a gaze for a torturous moment and just when the emotion seemed about to break free—just when she thought she would crumple and tell him the truth—his shoulders came down.

"No, I wouldn't ask you to do that." He sauntered toward the stall. "Tell Cait to set my place. I'll be along soon."

Returning to the house, Maddy kept her pace steady. *Don't think about what just happened. Don't give in to the tears.* But she *couldn't* keep her mind blank or the sense of devastation from creeping higher, tighter. She simply couldn't believe it. It was as if all her life she'd known every shade of blue and today she'd discovered she was color-blind. How had she gotten it so wrong? She'd been slow to come around, but last night…last night she'd *trusted* him. Truly believed there was so much more to Jack Prescott than arrogance and irresistible blistering charm.

But it seemed he'd meant what he said literally.

One night. Just one night.

That his conscience bit a little—that he couldn't quite meet her eyes—didn't mean his dismissive treatment of her hurt any less. With her blinders off, she shouldn't be surprised.

He'd kissed her in the moonlight when he'd been involved with Tara. No doubt there'd been women before his attractive neighbor. Who would come after *her?* She still believed he'd loved his wife but, clearly, now he was a rich, handsome bachelor, doing what rich, handsome bachelors did best.

Entertaining himself. Filling in time.

Inside the house, Maddy dragged herself to the nursery. When she pushed the partly-opened door the rest of the way, her blood froze in her veins. She'd walked into her worst nightmare.

Beau was awake, cooing in his crib. Nell was up on her hind legs, her black-and-white back hunched and front paws on the lower rail. Her long nose was thrust through the rungs.

Beau squealed and, horror-daze broken, Maddy rushed forward, all those faded memories from half a lifetime ago suddenly pulsing and hideously real. Discovered, Nell dropped and, tail between her legs, trotted off to the far corner before Maddy could rip her away.

"Get out of here," she growled through bared teeth.

Her heart was smashing through her ribs, her fingers tingled, her hands, her arms…they were losing their strength. As she glared at the dog, ready to physically throw her out of the room, Maddy tried to catch her breath.

She clung to the crib before her legs could give way. And still the collie stalked her with those deadly dark eyes.

Maddy hissed, "What are you staring at?"

Like a prowling wolf, Nell inched forward and, remembering those scars, Maddy exploded. "Get out! *Get out!*"

The baby wailed. Cait rushed in, Jack a heartbeat behind. The housekeeper threw a frantic look around while Jack strode to the center of the room, his fists clenched and gaze killer fierce.

"What the hell's going on?"

Maddy flapped her hand at Nell. "That-that *dog* shouldn't be in here alone with the baby. Her teeth were an inch from his arm. Dogs are unpredictable, Jack." Sometimes they were savage.

While Maddy scooped Beau from the crib and held him close, Cait's flushed face calmed and she came slowly forward.

"But Nell wouldn't hurt the bairn, Maddy."

Maddy's heart was bursting through her chest. "No one knows that."

The dog that had attacked her had been a family pet. She'd told Jack last night. He'd seen the scars. He'd said he'd understood—understood everything.

Or would he pretend as if none of that had happened, the same way he'd wanted to ignore her in the stables just moments ago?

But when he moved forward—when he put his hand over hers where she held the baby's head close—a static flicker of what they'd known together only hours before zoomed back.

His deep voice was low and gentle. "Maddy…honey… you're overreacting."

Maddy wanted to laugh. *She* was overreacting? He was

the one who wanted to lock everyone away behind these beastly remote station walls.

When he brought her close and urged her hot cheek to rest against his chest, she blinked several times. Concentrating on her breathing, on slowing her heartbeat, the dots before her eyes dispersed and, after a short time, most sped away. Nell lay in the corner, tail to the wall, ears down and head flat on her paws. Maddy swayed, leaned more against Jack and the tingling in her limbs began to fade.

She was stressed. Too much emotion. Too many memories stirred. Didn't change the fact that she would never allow Nell to come so close to Beau again, particularly when the baby was alone. Nothing would change her mind about that, and if anyone thought that was paranoid—tough luck.

But as Jack eased the baby from her arms and Cait called Nell out of the nursery, Maddy filled her lungs with a shuddering breath and the harrowing truth descended.

What could she do about it? If Beau was her child…

But he wasn't. She had as little say in Beau's life now as she had a week ago. *Less.* And the longer she stayed and had to swallow that reality, the more frustrated and upset she'd become.

Jack had been blunt but also spot-on. The decision was up to her but maybe it would be better better for everyone if she left and never came back.

Ten

In his lifetime, Jack had been to hell and back. Determined to find and sustain the strength he'd needed, most of the day he'd ridden the endless Leadeebrook plains on Herc's back. He'd returned to the homestead calm, cold and resolute.

But moments ago, when he'd taken Beau from Maddy and left her to wash her face and settle down before dinner, he'd been shell-shocked. The weight of the realization was like a stake being thrust into the heart. He was responsible, no one else, for her meltdown.

If she thought she'd fooled him in the stables into thinking their night together had meant little more than an adventurous fling on the side, she was mistaken. If she thought he didn't understand about Nell tonight in the nursery, after seeing those scars, of course he did. But, as harsh as he might've sounded, he meant what he'd said.

Soon her time here would be reduced to a quaint story

retold over Friday night cocktails. *He* would be the one left to make decisions for Beau and, damn right, he trusted Nell. More than he'd trust the drug addicts and pimps who trawled Sydney's King's Cross in broad daylight.

Forget about meltdowns and hurt feelings. Madison Tyler would always find fault with his world and he with hers. Fair enough, she was locked into her life and her future. She wanted to leave here to get back to it. Pity was she couldn't see what she set her compass by.

After their talk last night in Clancy, it was clear her main motivation in her job was her desire to prove herself to her father. Maddy wanted her father, as well as herself, to know she was strong. Strong enough to battle and survive anything.

Hell, who was he fooling? He was no better. He was as stubborn as she was. Worse.

Grumbling to himself, Jack carefully lay the baby down on the changing table. Beau wasn't his usual chirpy self either. After making a silly sound, Jack blew a raspberry on the baby's tummy and was rewarded by having his hair pulled by its roots. Little monkey.

Yep, he and Beau James would be happy here. People might call him a wealthy recluse behind his back, but so what? He wasn't budging, just like Maddy wasn't giving up Sydney or her dad.

Jack sprinkled powder, slipped on the diaper, smoothed over the tabs.

When an hour later, Maddy hadn't emerged from her room, Cait ventured in with a small plate of supper. Jack wasn't too hungry either, but he made a show for Cait's sake then took Beau out onto the veranda. He settled down on a chair with the baby on his lap. They were both keeping watch over another peaceful night when Snow Gibson rode up.

With that notorious bow-legged stride, Snow ascended the steps, found a beer in the outside fridge, tickled Beau's chin then pulled up a seat.

Jack said, "Missed you at supper." Snow had always joined him and Cait for Sunday dinner at the homestead.

"I sent word to Cait I wouldn't make it tonight."

"She said. What's up?"

Snow chugged on his beer then concentrated on the horizon.

"When I was your age, Jum, I was hop scotching around the place. Got all the way over to Western Australia one year. Sold carpet in Adelaide for a spell. Alice Springs was blasted hot but I wouldn't give it back for a row of Sundays. My only regret is that I didn't find a good woman, one to have that family with." He grinned over. "Maybe it's not too late."

Rearranging Beau, Jack shifted up in his chair. This sounded serious. "What's going on?"

"The bush is in my blood, but I'm too young to hide away, dig a hole and die just yet."

Jack caught on and he grinned. "And I am, too, right?"

"What you have here won't go away." Beau received an earnest tip of his head. "You want to take that boy of yours and do some living. You're a rich man. Some'd say filthy rich. Put that money to good use. Get a life."

Snow stood, finished his beer, hitched up his jeans and headed down the steps.

Jack watched his friend mount and ride away. When he looked down, Beau was asleep. He eased up and headed for the nursery.

He appreciated the concern but Snow didn't have his facts straight. He wasn't *dying* here. His aim was to give

Beau a safe upbringing. And he wasn't about to marry Maddy and have a family, if that was the hint.

Sure, the attraction that zapped between them couldn't be mistaken and, certainly, Beau loved Maddy. But the gulf that ran between them was as wide as the Murray. He was done thinking about it. Done mulling over the things that were better left to lie.

The kitchen was empty. Cait must've taken herself upstairs to bed. Jack entered the darkened nursery but stopped when he saw Maddy curled up in a corner sofa chair. A light blanket was cocooned around her chin. Her wrist, drooped over the arm of the chair, as well as her breathing, said she was sound asleep.

Her hair was a pale shimmering river spilling over her shoulder and he had to curb the impulse to settle Beau down then quietly carry her off to his bed and make love to her the way his body begged him to. But that wouldn't change the fact she'd be gone tomorrow.

Would she come back?

After today? Not likely.

He'd make sure she saw Beau if ever he landed in Sydney. But one day—and probably soon—Maddy would have her own family. She would be a prize for any man. She'd remember Dahlia's child fondly. Hopefully remember their night fondly, too. He always would.

Jack laid Beau in his bed and headed for the door. But then he stopped, frowned and turned back.

He couldn't say where the thought sprang from. He was certain in no possible way would it work. But she did love that baby, and last night proved that they were compatible, in the bedroom as well as intellectually. He knew deep down that advertising wasn't her thing, it was her father's.

What if he asked her to stay?

* * *

When Maddy's eyes dragged open, she wasn't sure of the time.

Rubbing her face, she sharpened her gaze and honed in on the window. Still dark, although a streaking mist hinted at the coming dawn. She straightened, winced. Someone had used her back as a pretzel.

The outline of Beau's crib cleared out of the shadows and her mind slotted up a gear. Twenty-four hours ago she'd been in Clancy, drifting off in that big beautiful bed, a satisfied smile on her face. Jack's arms had kept her so warm and close. Yesterday afternoon the illusion had been shattered.

Clenching her teeth against the crick in her spine, she moved to the crib.

She'd made a fool of herself over Nell. She had no say, no power here. Now there was nothing left for her but to escape. And yet what she wouldn't give to be here with Beau. To be here for him. There were women who'd had to give up their children at birth, or lost them in custody battles or to illness. To accidents. What Jack had endured when he'd lost his unborn baby had to be far worse than this.

On the brighter side there was every likelihood she'd see Beau again. When things settled between her and Jack, she'd contact him, ask when he was coming down to Sydney next. And if he stuck to his agoraphobic routine and refused to leave this place…

Well, she'd simply have to set pride aside and knock on his door. But the dust needed to settle first. Her mission had been to deliver Beau and make certain he was happy. She had and he was. As much as it tore her in two, it was time to move on. The text she received last night from her father confirmed it.

See you tomorrow. First thing.

After tugging the blanket up around sleeping Beau's back, she moved to her room next door to pack. She started to toss her ruined Keds in the wastebasket. She didn't want them dirtying up her suitcase. Instead she slipped them on. She'd get rid of them when she got home.

Dressed in jeans and a simple T-shirt, she'd finished swooping her hair up in a high ponytail when she heard something in the next room. Beau. At least an hour before he usually woke. Did he sense something off-kilter this morning?

He was crying softly by the time she collected his warm little body in her arms. Patting his back, she crooned close to his ear. "Hey, little guy. You hungry already?"

Beau's brow lowered, he tried to smile but he rubbed his eye with a tiny fist and grumbled again.

Jack appeared in the doorway. His alert gaze shot from the baby to her. He held up a bottle.

"I was up. It's warm."

She smiled and a part of her knew in the end everything would be all right. It had to be, for Beau's sake. She couldn't afford to blubber or be sullen or even cringe at the performance she'd made last night. Beau would sense the vibes and his welfare counted way and beyond anything else.

Maddy's insides clenched as she held him tighter still.

Ten minutes from now the cab would be here. But this wasn't like saying goodbye to Dahlia that black morning. Not like her mother telling her to be good before the bedroom door closed and she heard her father cry.

Maddy nuzzled into Beau's softness and baby scent and swallowed the tears.

I'm going to see you again. I promise, it won't be forever.

Jack's deep voice broke into her thoughts. "Sure I can't drive you in?"

"I'd rather—" Her words choked off and she cleared her throat. "It'll be easier."

He exhaled. Nodded. "Want a coffee? Pot's brewed."

"I'll get one at the airport."

He nodded again. Slid a foot back. "I'll get your bags."

She siphoned in a calming breath. A few minutes and then she'd be gone. From Beau. From Jack. From this place she hadn't liked yet over time had grown, in some way, attached to.

When Beau whimpered, Maddy sucked it up and put a carefree note into her voice.

"It's okay, baby." She pressed her lips to his brow. "Everything'll be okay. I promise, I promise."

She stopped. Frowned. Her head slowly drew away before she kissed his brow again. It was warm. Warmer than warm.

Jack had moved off down the hall. Striding out, she called him. "Jack!"

He spun around and must have seen the worry on her face and shot straight back.

She ran a hand over the baby's brow. "He's hot. Feel." He cupped Beau's face and his eyes darkened. "Maybe he's teething early. I have baby Tylenol in his bag."

At the same time Jack's gaze shot to the changing table, to the bag, Nell materialized out of nowhere. When the dog leaped up on the table, Maddy's stretched nerves snapped clean through. But before she could act and chase the dog out, Nell gripped the bag handles between her teeth, jumped down and trotted over.

Maddy's jaw dropped. "How did…?" She gaped at Jack. "She knows what we said?"

"Sometimes I think she has a better vocabulary than I do."

Beau began to grizzle and cry, his dear face crumpling and turning beet-red. A bizarre thought struck but Maddy couldn't shake it. Had Nell sensed Beau wasn't well last night? Was that why she'd poked her nose in? To check? Maybe she was trying to tell them something now.

Maddy reached to grip Jack's arm. "We should get him to a doctor."

But he was already halfway down the hall. To get the keys to his truck? She examined Beau, checking his face, his neck for rashes or spots. There were so many deadly viruses around.

Hearing Jack's muffled voice, she edged down the hall. He paced the kitchen, cell phone to his ear.

"Dr. Le Monde?" He drove a hand through his hair and, frowning deeply, nodded at the floor. "Yes, it's urgent."

Eleven

Help arrived within the hour.

Dr. Le Monde took Beau's temperature, checked for rashes and other signs of bacterial infection. He concluded Beau's fever was due to a viral infection. A common cold.

From a separate bag, the doctor revealed a piece of equipment—a vaporizer.

Standing beside the crib, Maddy watched over Beau, who was drifting off to sleep after a dose of medicine.

"I had one of those when I was young," she said. "It moistens the air. Helps your nose and lungs keep clear."

Le Monde's kind brown eyes glowed with approval. "Correct. It'll make things a little easier for him these next few days." The doctor put his hand on her shoulder. "Keep up his fluids. Cool boiled water in between feedings. Acetaminophen every four hours. He'll be irritable but fine soon enough." He spoke to Jack. "Call if you have any concerns—" he lifted his bike helmet off the floor by the door "—and I'll race straight back out."

Jack saw the doctor off. The bike roared away while Maddy patted Beau's head with a cool cloth. Her fingers brushed his flushed cheek and a fountain of love drew a soft smile across her face.

She would do anything to take his pain. He could never know how much she cared. How much he was loved.

Jack returned and set up the vaporizer. Beau was almost asleep by the time he switched the device on and stood beside her, gazing down on the baby in his crib as did she.

After a comfortable moment, he said in a hushed voice, "He seems better."

Beau's heavy eyes had drooped closed a final time and Maddy exhaled. "Thank heaven. But we're in for a sleepless night or two."

His hand shifted on the crib rail, brushed hers, and a frisson of awareness set light to her nerve endings, reminding her of everything she was so desperate to forget. She demanded that her feet move a little to the left. They didn't listen. If she weren't so stern, they might have moved to the right, closer to Jack's natural heat.

The whir of the vaporizer filtered through the room and she drew the sheet over Beau's shoulder at the same time Jack brushed a curl from his forehead. Their hands touched, lingered, before they each drew away.

"You've missed your flight," he said.

"Guess I have."

But she wouldn't think about Pompadour Shoes or her father's disappointment. She only wanted to soak up the vision of Beau slipping into a peaceful sleep and the knowledge that his illness wasn't serious. She hated to think of the time they might've spent in a city triage unit in similar circumstances. Not that Jack might not resort to putting his fist through a wall if he thought it'd get someone's attention.

Now, however, he was almost meek, although she sensed that intense inherent power rippling beneath the calm.

His thumb tapped the crib rail. "You want to call your father?"

"Soon."

"What'll you tell him?"

"That I couldn't get away." She tried to dredge up an appropriate emotion but in the end she shrugged. "He'll need to hand over the account to someone else."

Jack rolled back his shoulders. "I can get you there in—"

"I'm staying." But she tempered her determined tone with a smile. "No arguments." And before he could insist, she added, "I'm sure."

After three days and nights with little sleep for the adults, Beau's temperature was back to normal, his chest was clear, and his cooing and laughter once again filled the house. Maddy glowed inside when she heard it. Again she was reminded how very precious it was to know that those you loved were well.

Thursday, as Maddy gave Beau his evening bath, she pondered over the Tyler Advertising presentation scheduled for the next day.

Was she sad she wouldn't be there? Mad? Disappointed in herself?

Ultimately she was proud she'd made the right choice. The only choice. These past few days her place had been here with this child. His health and happiness were the only things that truly mattered.

When Cait came in, Beau kicked his heels, splashing water over the table and floor. Chuckling, Cait rustled a towel out from under the table.

"He's certainly got his energy back."

Maddy scooped him out of the baby bath and Cait pat-dried every inch of him. When Maddy took over with the talc, Cait asked, "Have you heard from your father?"

Maddy sighed and shook her head.

Cait had become something of a confidante. Maddy had confessed a little of her feelings for Jack, more about Beau and had also admitted how disappointed her father would be that she'd stayed when she'd promised to go home. Cait had been so supportive, like Maddy imagined her mother would have been. She would never forget this woman's kindness. She would be sad to leave it behind.

Cait flicked out a new diaper. "Well, we all three thank you for staying. It was a brave move. One you didn't need to make and yet you did. Give him time. Your father'll see that, too."

Jack tiptoed in on his socks. When he saw Beau awake and ready for some fun, he cruised over and pumped his little legs, making him giggle. Maddy stepped aside while Jack prepared to fold Beau into his PJs. He'd gotten pretty good at handling those tiny snaps.

Cait put away the talc then laced her fingers over her waist.

"Now everyone's here," she said clearly to get their attention, "I've been on the phone to Beatrice Claudia. She runs the hotel in town," she explained for Maddy's benefit. "Her poor canary fell off his perch this morning and she's beside herself. I offered to come stay the night. Share some sherry. Maybe talk her into buying another bird. No one wants to live alone."

Maddy thought she saw something more flash behind

Cait's eyes but then the housekeeper straightened and cleared her throat.

"Anyways," Cait went on, "the crisis here is over. Dinner's cooked, so if you don't mind, Jock, I'll take the truck to town tonight."

"You know where the keys are," he offered. "Give my condolences to Mrs. Claudia."

Cait caught Maddy's eye before she headed off. "Don't expect me home before noon."

Two hours later Beau was asleep.

Maddy enjoyed a long soapy shower then found Jack, equally exhausted and freshly scrubbed, sprawled out on a sofa in the living room. Maddy fell back into the cushions alongside of him.

She sighed. "I could sleep for a week."

Jack groaned. "Starting now."

Maddy was zoned out, eyes closed, remembering the rosy tint in Beau's healthy cheeks tonight, when Jack's question took her by surprise.

"When will you be heading back?"

She blinked across at him. "You're that eager to get rid of me?"

Jack sat straighter, ready to deny it, but when Maddy only grinned, his shoulders went down and he smiled, too.

These past days the atmosphere had changed between them again. He was still dynamic and gorgeous—nothing could ever change that. But they'd worked so closely to make sure Beau was comfortable and on the mend. There'd been no time or energy to hold grudges over what had gone before.

She wanted to move on from their awkward discussion in the stables and had all but convinced herself that Nell would only ever protect the baby; she certainly seemed tuned in to the humans around her and, rather than let the past cloud the present, Maddy decided she should take some solace in that.

Strange to admit but, after these few days, Maddy felt almost at home here and felt close to comfortable again with Jack. He'd done everything he could to help and she appreciated it. Maybe it was time to put her changed feelings into words. No time like the present.

Sitting an arm's length away, she turned to him. He turned at the same time. Their eyes connected and Maddy felt drawn to him as she had been so many times before. It was as if her body knew the danger to Beau was past and now it was time to get back to other unresolved matters.

But that wasn't happening. To go there again with Jack would only complicate what had been settled well enough. They'd shared one night. She wasn't about to make it two, even if she suspected Cait had made herself scarce for precisely that reason.

When his gaze dropped to her mouth, she felt more than saw him lean nearer. A violent tug of war kicked off in her mind, in her heart, and, panicking, she flung up both hands.

"Jack, please...let's not do this."

He stopped, nodded gravely. "You're right." He slid over. "Let's do this."

He dragged her against him and his mouth claimed hers. Astonished as well as instantly, unspeakably aroused, she pushed against his chest but Jack didn't budge. In fact, he drew her closer, kissed her deeper, and soon, rather than pushing, her hands were flexing and rubbing, wanting to get beneath his shirt.

She was barely aware of being carried from the lounge to his room. When he set her on her feet, their clothes came off in a flurry while they twirled and stumbled their way over toward his bed. His mouth on hers, he blindly threw back the covers and, breathing labored, swept her up and laid her down, not in a gentle way.

Curled over her in the shadows, his shoulders expanded as he inhaled a hungry breath and apologized. "I'm being too rough."

She hauled him down. "I won't break."

Their mouths crashed together again, and every time his tongue swept around hers, it stroked and teased the wild surge building inside her, a delicious quickening of her blood that left her panting and clinging to his arms, to his hips. When his erection stabbed her belly, she threw him off and swung on top, her thighs spread and clenched over his. Hair spilling across her face, she slowly arched above him and, teasing, grazed the sensitive tips of her breasts over his chest.

It was as if she were acting outside of herself. Released from their cage, her animal instincts had taken over and every part of her could focus only on satisfying the spiraling aching need he stoked so deep inside.

She'd never felt like this before. On fire. Everywhere. Incinerating.

His hot hands cupped her hips and shifted her up then ground her back down. His expression was an uneven mix of darkest lust and burning appreciation.

He craned up and wrapped his lips around one nipple. He tickled the tip with his tongue and, sighing, she gripped his head.

"Guess it's been building up," he murmured, tugging at her tender tip with his teeth.

She groaned and writhed. "Only to atomic proportions."

They rolled again and he pinned her beneath him.

When he entered her—when she felt him fill her until he hit that throbbing unstable spot only he knew about—she gasped then bit her lip and focused. How could that wave reach so high so fast?

He moved again and she gazed up into his eyes with a helpless, keen fascination. All the fine pieces of the universe were hurtling toward her core. The sublime pressure was contracting around that single, bright pulsing light. When he hit that spot again—when he unleashed the critical power that made her so completely, purely his—she drove her spine into the mattress and cried out. A heartbeat later, he followed her over the edge.

When the stars faded, they were both damp with perspiration and out of breath. Yet, as she brushed the hair from her eyes, still humming all over, she had the urge to laugh. She'd never been so out of control in the bedroom. Never so out of control in her *life*. What a racket they'd made.

Thank God Beau was fast asleep and Cait wasn't around. Maddy hadn't known lovemaking could be so raw. So beyond anything she'd ever experienced.

After kissing her again—long and slow this time—Jack blew out a satiated breath. "We won't be able to get away with that kind of noise when he's older."

She went to agree but then the deeper meaning behind that statement soaked fully through. Fazed, she glanced across. His expression was easy yet half speculative.

He'd known what he said. How was she supposed to respond? Especially now when every fiber that made up her mind and body buzzed with such bone-deep satisfaction.

Where did they go from here? *How* did they go from here?

A noise filtered down the hall. They both stilled then sprang up.

"Beau." She flipped back the sheet. "I'll go check."

"You've barely left his side today. It's my shift." His finger stabbed the air. "That's an order."

She nodded and watched him drag on his shorts and stride away. She heard Beau squeak, the muffled rumble of Jack's voice. Then nothing. Slowly her muscles relaxed and she lay down again. Put her hand behind her head. Eventually closed her eyes.

She woke with a start and squinted at the luminous digital clock. After midnight.

She looked across and found she was alone in the bed. Where was Jack? How was Beau? She strained to hear. Had the baby had a relapse?

She swung Jack's shirt off the floor and, in a hurry, punched her arms through the sleeves. But the room was dark and unfamiliar. On her way to the door, she tripped over something that might have been a boot and landed hard against the drawers.

Pressing her lips together, she swore under her breath. *Damn.* Her little toe felt broken.

Rubbing her foot, gritting her teeth to control the pain, she slowly straightened. A stream of moonlight was beaming in through a crack in the curtain. On top of the drawers, illuminated, that silver framed photo leaped up to greet her. At the frame's base, a gold circle shone in the moonlight. Holding her breath, Maddy reached to touch…

A wedding ring.

She'd seen this photo the day she'd arrived but everything had moved so fast tonight, she hadn't thought about it when he'd swept her in here earlier. How would things have played out if she had remembered? Because now she didn't feel the least bit sexy or impulsive. She felt like an intruder, particularly given that Jack still wore the matching gold band around his neck.

His words echoed in her mind.

When he's older... Next time...

She wanted there to be a next time. And a next. But she didn't know how she felt about making love with a man who still considered himself married the way Jack so clearly did. She certainly wouldn't go there again with this photo watching over them.

A glow way off down the hall drew her eye. Giving her toe a final rub she limped toward it and eventually found herself in a room she hadn't entered before... A large and lavish yet strangely cozy library, with a vast collection of spines highlighted in crafted wood bookcases.

In the far corner, Jack sat on a couch holding a book. She recognized the cover. She had the same edition at home.

He glanced up and found a smile. "You were sleeping so soundly, I didn't expect you to wake."

"So you thought you'd catch a few chapters of *Jane Eyre?*"

He grinned. "Sue loved reading, like you." His gaze grew distant. "I figured I'd spend the rest of my days riding the plains during the day and looking over these spines at night."

Her gaze filtered over the rows and rows of books. All Sue's. Would she have liked Jack's wife? Maddy tugged the oversized shirt around her naked body more firmly. She wouldn't think about that just now.

She wandered over and took the book. "This is one of my favorites. The ending stays with you forever." The fierce patriarch had been reduced to rely upon the loyal governess.

When she flipped to the back cover, scanned the lines

and handed it back, he drew her down onto his lap and concentrated on the motion of curling hair behind her ear.

"Something Snow said the other night…it's making a lot of sense. We're good together, Maddy. Way better than good. And Beau needs a mother."

She predicted the bombshell about to hit. Overwhelmed, she lowered her lashes to hide her shock.

He was going to ask her to *marry* him? It was too amazing to contemplate. Just now she'd confirmed again in her mind that Jack still considered himself to be married. That he would always consider himself to be married to his deceased wife. Had she been wrong?

With a knuckle, he raised her chin and willed her to meet his somber gaze. "Maddy, I'm asking you to stay."

The words took a moment to sink in. *Not* a marriage proposal. He was asking her to move in. He'd said Beau needed a mother. He wanted her to pull up pegs in Sydney and replant them out here?

Her voice was a hoarse rasp. "You want me to live at *Leadeebrook?*"

An image of that photo sitting on his bedroom drawers swirled up and her mind's eye tunneled in on the delicate gold ring. Its larger twin lay shining on Jack's bare chest now.

Her gaze jumped from the ring to the wall of books—Sue's library. Sue's room. Sue's house.

She swallowed against a tight ache in her throat. "What about your wife?"

His eyes narrowed, as though he suspected she'd suffered a memory loss. "Sue's dead."

"But she isn't to you. Not here." Her palm covered the left side of his chest, her fingers brushing the wedding band.

The questions in his eyes cleared even as his jaw tightened almost imperceptibly. "You want marriage?"

"Oh, Jack, it's not about that." The way she felt—the problem this "offer" posed—it wasn't that simple.

Although she couldn't deny that the past few days, when she'd seen Jack being so good with Beau, she'd imagined them as a family. Perhaps with another child or two. But the more she'd thought about it, the more ridiculous it had seemed. First up, where would they live? His world or hers?

Yet in Jack's mind he'd settled that point. He'd asked her to stay here. With the dust and the horse hair and the flies. Of course, there was a lot to like, as well…the history, the sunsets, the peace. But her life was so firmly entrenched in the city, she could think of only one response to his question.

"Why don't you both come and live in Sydney?"

He winced. "You know the answer to that."

She pushed off his lap. "Explain it to me."

"Sydney's fine. Beautiful city, as far as cities go. But it's not home."

"Not your home, but it's mine."

He stood, too. "I'm offering you a new home."

She didn't want a new home, not in the country a million miles from the nearest mall. Away from her friends. Her job. Her father.

She stopped and, torn in two, squeezed shut her eyes.

But Beau was here. Jack, too.

Her stomach knotted and she covered her hot face. Oh God, she had to think. And her thoughts came back to that little boy. Jack was Beau's legal guardian. This was his home, like it or not. But one day he would grow into a teenager with a mind and a will of his own. Like Dahlia had.

"What about Beau?" she asked, dropping her hands. "What happens when he wants to see and live and experience life beyond these fences?" Did Jack want Beau to follow in his sister's drastic footsteps and run away?

"When the time comes, he'll have the best higher education available and that means Sydney." His hands found hers. "But Beau is a Prescott. A male descendant. I won't need to insist he stay because he belongs here, same way I do, like his grandfather and his father before him."

She barely contained an astonished huff. "And the women don't get a choice." When he released her hands as if they'd burned, she hurried on. "I want to be with you and Beau. But how can I say I'll stay when I have a whole life back home?"

He didn't look impressed. "A whole life."

"A job. Friends. You know." She shrugged, exasperated. "A life."

His shoulders squared and his eyes dulled. "Then you've answered my question."

A deep dark cavern open up inside her. Damn his arrogant streak. What made him think the world revolved around him? Didn't anyone else's feelings or background count?

"Why is it okay for you to dig your heels in and not me?"

Detached now, he collected the book off the couch. His voice was a low drawl. "You can do what you please."

Her mouth dropped open then she slowly shook her head. His about-face was so swift and definite, it left her dizzy. "I thought I could talk to you. Thought we were at last somewhere on the same page. But you haven't heard anything I've said." He was only prepared to listen to the voices of tradition and the past. All the ghosts that kept him here and wouldn't him let go.

He slotted the book away, ran his finger down the spine. "If your job is more important—"

"That's not fair."

He spun around. "It's not about being fair."

Maddy staggered back.

He was just like her father, implacable, and just as hard to please. She was sick of trying. Tired of playing everyone else's games.

"You might've put up your feet and retired, Jack, but I have a job, and it's full time."

He crossed his arms. "Is working for your father where you want to be?"

The question took her aback but she recovered. "It's no different than you insisting you belong here."

"I belong here because this is where my heart is. Is your heart in Tyler Advertising?"

"You grew up with shearers. I grew up with jingles and slogans. It's all I know. My father took the time to groom me." It's what she'd told herself for years, and yet now she knew she was trying to convince herself.

"Your father will still love you whether you work for him or not. You don't stop loving someone because they choose a different path from the one you'd wanted them to take."

"But you might stop talking to them." *Like you stopped talking to Dahlia.* And suddenly she had to know. She'd believed it a few days ago. Had things ever changed?

Despite shaking inside, she injected a note of calm into her voice. "Would you cut me off, Jack, if I walked away now?"

His eyes turned to ice. "You'd be the one leaving. Not me. I have no control over that."

Maddy held her stomach. How could she argue? It seemed useless to try.

Every day he lived regretting that he hadn't been able to control certain situations and people, and yet he'd let her walk away now without an argument. And if he thought that way, surely that validated what was obvious. Dreams were nice, but that's all they were. She didn't belong here. Even as much as she loved and wanted to be with Beau, there was simply too much against it.

Obviously Jack was of the same opinion because he drove both hands through his hair, holding them there before his arms dropped to his sides. When he looked at her again, his face was blank.

"So what about Beau?" he asked.

Her gaze landed on the Bible on a shelf behind him and a well-known story came to mind.

"Say I did stay. Beau and I would grow even closer." When she waited, he conceded with a curt nod. "If it didn't work out between us and I decided to leave, would you consider sharing custody?"

His presence seemed to swell and intensify before her eyes, like an otherworldly force taking on immeasurable power. But as quickly as it had surfaced, that tension left his body and a different strain appeared.

Stubborn pride.

"No," he said, no hint of remorse in his voice. "I'll never give him up."

Twelve

Jack was not in a good mood.

Two nights ago, he and Maddy had come to an understanding. Of sorts.

He'd dealt his hand and had asked her to stay. She'd countered with the obvious: she couldn't give up her lifestyle. Why was he surprised? You could take the girl out of the city, but…

He kicked his heels into Herc and the horse galloped harder.

Dammit, he was better off without her.

The sun was rising as he rode Herc into the yard. He yanked up so hard on the reins, hooves ploughed up a swirling cloud of red dust that filled his lungs. He swung out of the saddle and his boots hit the ground with a thump.

If he were lucky he'd have missed Maddy's early departure. That would be best. Everything there was to say had been said. He had Beau. His memories. His station. If he had to say goodbye to her… Ah hell, he'd said goodbyes before.

He clapped Herc's flank and the horse reared off into the stables.

When he spun around, she stood at the bottom of the steps. Jeans, white top, pale hair pulled off her flawless beautiful face…so beautiful, he could barely breathe.

Emotion—both raw and bleak—booted him in the chest. Coming back to earth, he stuck his hat more firmly on his head and strode over.

"Thanks," he said formally, "for staying with Beau when he needed you."

"Thanks," she said, just as blandly, "for letting me stay."

Neither looked away. It was as if whoever broke first, lost. Or maybe it was because this was truly the end but there was still that maddening urge to carry her back inside and lock her in until she came around. A hundred years ago he might've done it.

The thought was still hovering when the sound of an engine in the quiet morning pulled his head around. A dusty Yellow cab groaning up the ruts.

Cait appeared at the top of the steps, the baby propped in one arm. She descended as if she were performing a funeral march. On top of everything, he didn't need that. The cab braked at the same time Cait joined them.

She tried her best to smile. "Baby Beau wants to say goodbye."

Maddy's slim nostrils flared but she managed to smile over the moisture filling her eyes. She cupped the baby's face, her hand pale against his cheek, and brushed her lips over his brow. "Be good, Beau darling." Jack caught her barest whisper, "Remember me."

She didn't look at Jack as she turned toward the opened cab door and slid inside. And then she was gone. In the cab, down that endless track. She didn't look back. Not once.

Cait lifted sympathetic eyes to his but Jack only growled beneath his breath. He wanted to take Beau from her, comfort him—feel the connection—but he wasn't sure that was such a good idea right now.

Instead he stormed up the steps. He strode into his room and slammed the door, so hard that the walls rattled. The photo on the drawers wobbled and crashed to the floor. The ring fell, too, bouncing with a tinkle on the wood. Then it rolled over the timber boards until it stopped and dropped at his boots.

A burning arrow tore through his heart and he flinched. Hunching over, Jack pressed the butts of his hands hard against his stinging eyes. Every muscle in his body felt wound tight enough to snap. He wanted to yell. Wanted to put his fist through that door.

He wanted back what he'd lost.

After a few moments, he blew out a shuddering breath and hunkered down. He reached for the wedding band. The gold felt warm, felt familiar. Keeping it close to him these past years...was it commitment?

Or was it time?

Jack wasn't sure how long he sat on the end of the bed, holding that ring and working through things in his mind. When Cait tapped on the door and asked if he was okay, he told her not to worry.

His hands were steady when he unclasped the chain from around his neck. He moved across the room, collected the photo off the floor and slid open the top drawer. Closing his eyes, remembering and cherishing it all, he kissed the frame then put the photo and both rings safely away.

Thirteen

Maddy's cell call connected at the same time the regional airport loudspeaker announced her flight was ready to board.

She'd checked in her luggage, had grabbed that coffee. Now she needed to do something that would lift a great weight. She was tired and done with carrying it.

Her father's smooth voice filtered down the line from Sydney.

"Madison, you said it was urgent. I meant to get back to you sooner." Papers shuffled. "I've been busy."

On Monday she'd left a message that she didn't know when she could get back, that the baby needed her and he should find a replacement account executive for the Pompadour account. A lot had happened since then.

"Dad, I need to resign."

"I've already taken care of that. Gavin Sheedy's taken on the Pompadour account—"

"I need to resign from Tyler Advertising."

Maddy pressed her lips together as the silence at the other end stretched out.

Drew Tyler's voice was deep and wary. "You're in love with that man, aren't you? I spoke with a colleague the other day. He said he saw you at a—"

She cut in again. "Jack Prescott has nothing to do with my decision." And as the words left her mouth she knew it was true. "Daddy, you love what you do. I wanted so badly to make you proud. I wanted to prove to us both I could make it." Be strong. Survive. No matter what. "But since I've been gone…" There was no easy way to say it. She sucked in a breath. "Advertising isn't what I'm meant to do. It's not who I want to be."

"I see." His tone was reflective, calm. "And what is it you do want to do?"

Her gaze wandered around the busy terminal, people arriving from exotic destinations, families flying off to find new adventures. She saw the shining opportunities and experiences glowing around them like auras.

She shucked back her shoulders and felt herself grow. "I want to travel."

When her father laughed, not in derision but an uncommonly merry sound, she almost fell over.

"Sweetheart, that's a marvelous idea. I wish now I'd had time off when you were younger to take you myself. And when you get back—"

"You're not angry?" Maddy shook herself. He'd spent so much time helping her, coaching her.

"Honey, advertising can be cutthroat. At least it is at Tyler. It's not you. Never was."

The rest of his words faded. Maddy had pivoted around. Now her attention was hooked on the terminal's automatic sliding doors—or rather, on who was striding through them.

The air left her lungs in a whoosh.

"Jack...?"

His purposeful gait pulled up. Long denim-clad legs braced apart, he cast a hawkish gaze around. The thunder in his face said he was ready, and able, to tear the place apart if need be.

Maddy swallowed to wet her dry throat. "Dad, I need to call you back."

She didn't hear the reply. The phone dropped from her ear at the same time Jack spotted her. He marched over with such masterful purpose, Maddy almost wanted to hide. What was the matter? What on earth had she done? Was something wrong with Beau?

He stopped a foot away. Before she could think, he drew her in hard against him and kissed her—kissed her with what felt like everything his soul could gather and give.

One hot hand cupping her neck, the other winging her shoulder in, his caress penetrated every aching, wanting layer—of her mind, of her heart, of her spirit. She'd schooled herself to accept she would never feel the divine skill of his mouth on hers again. She'd fortified her willpower and was determined not to break and go back.

But as the kiss deepened and the pounding of his heartbeat melded with hers, Maddy couldn't bury the truth. She loved this man. Like no woman had ever loved a man before. Every day, every minute of her life, a part of her would be with him. How she wished she'd met him first.

As thrilling as this hurricane display of affection was,

a man couldn't be in love with two women at the same time. Although she couldn't think badly of Sue, it broke her inside to know she wasn't the blue ribbon one.

The kiss broke softly. She went to speak, but his fingertip touched her still-wet lips.

"I've tortured myself," he said. "I can't count the times I've asked why people I love keep leaving me. Maddy, you had the answer."

"Jack, I *so* don't have any answers."

She tried to wiggle free—nothing could change her mind, make this work—but his hold remained firm.

"You told me that night in Clancy. What happened in the past was out of my hands. This isn't. I've made mistakes before. No doubt I'll make more in the future. But letting you walk out of my life won't be one of them." He lifted her chin and scanned her eyes. "I love Leadeebrook. But I love you a thousand times more. Whatever it takes to keep you in my life, I'll do it. If you want to live in the city, we'll do that. And we'll live every day to the fullest. We have enough money to live three lifetimes in luxury."

Maddy's jaw unhinged. Her brain was stuck way back.

"You'd *sell* Leadeebrook?"

"If it means having you—" he smiled with his eyes "—in an instant. I'd shut down. Closed myself off. You and Beau opened me up again—to hope. To *feeling*. To all the things that make living worthwhile."

When Maddy grew dizzy, she remembered to breathe.

He was *deluded*. Must have fallen off his horse and bumped his head. He couldn't know what he was saying.

"I—I can't let you sell." That sheep station was a part of him, as much as an arm or a leg.

But he seemed to think her confusion was funny. He chuckled. "Don't worry. I've never thought more clearly in my life." His smile changed. "Driving here I wondered… Do you think Dahlia might've hoped for something like this?"

"You mean for us to—"

She couldn't say it. If she did, this wild wonderful dream would dissolve and she'd wake up.

But he nodded and said the words for her. "For us to fall in love. Maybe Dahlia could see the three people she loved most in the world finding happiness together."

Tears raced from the corners of her eyes as her gaze slipped to the open V of his shirt. The chain was gone. She honed in on his naked left hand, just in case, and a sob caught high in her throat.

He'd put away the ring. He wanted to move on? Could he honestly, truly give his heart to another woman…to her?

Another possibility came to mind and her throat swelled.

"Are you doing this for Beau…so he'll have a mother?"

Somehow she couldn't hate him if he was.

He came close and his warm breath murmured against her temple. "I love you, Maddy. Please…let me love you. Say you'll marry me."

Something in his voice, in the way his lips brushed her skin, told her it was safe. Not just for now but forever. And suddenly it didn't matter where they lived or what they did. As long as they were together. The three of them together from now on.

Her cheeks were hot and wet. Her voice was a desperate, elated whisper needing to be heard.

"Yes, I'll marry you. I love you, Jack." Her breath caught

on a joy-filled laugh. "I want to be with you so much. Wherever that is. Every day. Every night."

When she answered him again with a kiss that was created from deepest faith and sealed with the promise of everlasting love, smiling into her eyes, Jack swept up his bride-to-be.

And took her home to Leadeebrook.

Epilogue

Maddy's silk gloved hands tugged back on the ribbon reins and Herc's brief journey came to an end.

Pink-and-white petals littered the outdoor aisle, which led to a gazebo laced with climbing roses and gold satin bows. Friends, seated on either side, kept their rapt, so-happy-for-you faces turned her way. But Maddy's gaze was drawn to only one.

Jack's shoulders in that crisp dark jacket had never looked broader. She already felt the rasp of his freshly shaven jaw, could already smell the masculine scent that made her feel so warm and prized. His eyes were dancing. Dancing with love. The same unique love she'd felt thrive these past nine months. Today she could barely hold back from shouting and telling the world.

Drew Tyler, in his morning suit, took her hand and helped the bride from her sidesaddle onto an elevated platform then down two steps to the lawn.

"I've never seen you look more beautiful." Her father's eyes glistened as he smiled. "I'm so pleased for you, sweetheart. Your mother would be, too."

Emotion filling her throat, she squeezed her father's hand while three bridesmaids fussed to arrange her sweeping train. Her wedding gown's white silk and organza bodice hugged to the hips before flaring out into a fairy-tale skirt, which was highlighted by scatterings of sequined leaves gold flecks that echoed her fiancé's eyes.

Adoring eyes that were pinned on her.

The music swelled. Her father looped her arm through his and Maddy closed her eyes. Her mother and Dahlia were close. She felt their wishes for happiness drifting over her.

Her father whispered near her ear, "You ready?"

Smiling, she opened her eyes and together they took the first measured step.

Standing beside Jack, Snow looked splendid in a black-tie dinner suit. He'd even trimmed his beard. As he winked at her, Maddy's gaze, through the fine net of her veil, tracked over to Cait, sitting up front. Year-old Beau was perched quietly on her lap, his big eyes glued on "Mummy." Nell sat beside them, well-behaved, too, wearing a pale pink tutu Cait must have organized for the occasion.

Then the music was fading and she was standing beside Jack, tears of pure joy misting her eyes. He'd never looked more handsome. More proud. Carefully he folded back her veil and the minister raised his book.

When the vows and rings were exchanged, Beau clapped harder than anyone. He jumped off Cait's lap and, blond curls bouncing, scampered up in his tuxedo playsuit to hug his parents' legs extra-tight.

The wedding breakfast was served in a twinkling marquee with a billowing white silk ceiling. When Jack led her to the dance floor for the bridal waltz, Maddy wanted to warn her husband that she hadn't forgotten her promise: today she'd ridden a horse and changed her name. He needed to get ready to dance the polka.

But she had far more important news and she couldn't hold back a moment more.

Her gaze on his bow tie, she ran her hand down his satin lapel. "There's something I need to tell you."

"News? I wonder if it's as good as mine. But you first."

She met his gaze. He looked so enthused, she smiled and tipped her head. "No, you."

"Snow and I've come up with an idea to turn Leadeebrook into a sheep station museum. We can dress it up for the public, have sheepdog shows, shearing displays, outback extravaganzas. You were right. This place is too special, has too much history, to let lie around and decay."

Maddy beamed and hugged his neck. Jack was kept busy enough with his investment portfolio as well as being a great dad to Beau, but some days she caught the restlessness in his eyes. This museum plan was exactly what he needed.

But they spent a good deal of time in Sydney now, coming back here to Leadeebrook for quiet times in between. It wasn't a compromise on either one's part. They were simply enjoying the best both their worlds had to offer.

"Does that mean we'll be spending more time here than Sydney now?" she asked.

He dropped a kiss on her inside wrist. "We'll spend as much time here as you want." He grinned. "Although

Beau's social calendar is pretty full in Sydney. Play groups, swimming classes."

"He's a popular kid."

"With a popular and extremely beautiful mother." His forehead rested upon hers but as he rocked her around to the music, the laughter faded from his eyes. What replaced it made her heart swell and cheeks heat with that familiar desire she could never get enough of.

"Thank you for bringing me back to life," he murmured as wedding guests danced around them. "I love you so much, I just want to grab on and never let you go. In fact..." Taking her by surprise, he gripped her high on her waist and swung her in a circle so that her feet left the ground and her train flew out in a glittering white river around them.

She was laughing, out of breath, when he set her down. Giddy, she righted her diamond-and-pearl tiara. "We might need to go a little easy on that kind of spontaneous stuff for a while." When his brows knitted, questioning her, she teased, "Just for seven or eight months."

Jack's pupils dilated. Then his chest expanded to a breadth and width she hadn't witnessed before. He drove a hand through his hair and again.

"You mean you're..." His Adam's apple bobbed up and down. "You and I...Maddy...we're having a *baby?*"

She bit her lip but couldn't contain the ear to ear smile. "Uh-huh."

He whooped then dipped, about to grab and spin her around again. But he stopped then stepped back.

His smile disappeared. "Do you need to sit down?"

A flicker of unease brushed her stomach but she quickly assured him. "I'm fine. Fantastic. The doctor says everything's better than good." She held his hands, searched his eyes. "But if you want to postpone our honeymoon in Paris… I mean, if you're worried about me flying right now or anything…"

I'll understand.

He blinked slowly and a line creased between his brows.

"We've been to New York," he said, "Hawaii and New Zealand with Beau. I don't see why this little one can't experience France—" he settled his warm palm over her belly and grinned "—even if it's from in here."

Maddy flung her arms around him. He wasn't going to wrap her in cotton wool? Wasn't going to even hint that they should hibernate here at the station, at least until after the birth?

She pulled back. "Are you sure?"

"No. I'm positive." His strong arms gathered her in. "Know what I love most about you?"

"I think I do." Playful, she craned up and skimmed her adoring lips over his.

He chuckled and the rumble vibrated through to her bones. "Besides that."

"Tell me."

"I love that every day I discover something new and wonderful that only makes me love you more."

A surprise tear escaped and rolled down her cheek as his head slanted over hers. Their lips brushed again and again. After she murmured how much she loved him, too, she rested her cheek on his chest and contemplated their fabulous future together.

A cry of *"Dad-da!"* brought them to attention.

They turned. Cait was holding Beau. "Your son wants to dance."

Laughing, Jack scooped Beau onto the swing of his sleeve and Beau clapped his hands while Maddy welcomed the wonderful sense of completeness.

Contentment.

She'd always wanted to belong, but no one belonged to a job or address. Dancing with Jack and their son on their wedding day, with another beautiful baby on the way, Maddy knew exactly who she was and where she needed to be.

With her heart.

With her family.

Wherever their love was, God willing, so was she.

* * * * *

Harlequin offers a romance for every mood!
See below for a sneak peek from
our suspense romance line
Silhouette® Romantic Suspense.
Introducing HER HERO IN HIDING
by New York Times *bestselling author Rachel Lee.*

Kay Young returned to woozy consciousness to find that she was lying on a soft sofa beneath a heap of quilts near a cheerfully burning fire. When she tried to move, however, everything hurt, and she groaned.

At once she heard a sound, then a stranger with a hard, harsh face was squatting beside her. "Shh," he said softly. "You're safe here. I promise."

"I have to go," she said weakly, struggling against pain. "He'll find me. He can't find me."

"Easy, lady," he said quietly. "You're hurt. No one's going to find you here."

"He will," she said desperately, terror clutching at her insides. "He always finds me!"

"Easy," he said again. "There's a blizzard outside. No one's getting here tonight, not even the doctor. I know, because I tried."

"Doctor? I don't need a doctor! I've got to get away."

"There's nowhere to go tonight," he said levelly. "And if I thought you could stand, I'd take you to a window and show you."

But even as she tried once more to pull away the quilts, she remembered something else: this man had been gentle when he'd found her beside the road, even when she had kicked and clawed. He hadn't hurt her.

Terror receded just a bit. She looked at him and detected signs of true concern there.

The terror eased another notch and she let her head sag on the pillow. "He always finds me," she whispered.

"Not here. Not tonight. That much I can guarantee."

Will Kay's mysterious rescuer protect
her from her worst fears?
Find out in HER HERO IN HIDING
by New York Times *bestselling author Rachel Lee.*
Available June 2010, only from
Silhouette® Romantic Suspense.

HARLEQUIN®
Blaze™